murmur

TIM EARNSHAW

murmur

VICTOR GOLLANCZ
LONDON

A Gollancz Paperback Original
First published in Great Britain in 1999
by Victor Gollancz
An imprint of Orion Books Ltd,
Orion House, 5 Upper St Martin's Lane, London WC2H 9EA

A CIP catalogue record for this book is
available from the British Library.

ISBN 0 575 06616 4

Typeset by SetSystems Ltd, Saffron Walden, Essex
Printed and bound in Great Britain by
Clays Ltd, St Ives plc

Dedicated to
2008

I thank all my good friends, especially Udo, Louisa,
Claudia and Simon, Hugo, Dante, and Big George
and Little George

'You Need A Mess Of Help To Stand Alone'

Tim Earnshaw
Hollywood
February 1999

'Broken speech; speech broken by silence. To let the silence in is symbolism. "In symbol there is concealment yet revelation: here therefore, by Silence and by Speech acting together, comes a double significance."'

Carlyle quoted in Brown, *Love's Body*

Something Inaudible

I'm Outstanding

Nothing But Fear

I'm Happy

Everything Was Blurred

Answer Me

Like a Normal Guy

Dust

Still Feel Smart?

Perfect

Nothing But Shadows

All He Was

Paradise Fucked

Nothing

Half This

Hell

He's On Fire

Nothing

Something Inaudible

It was the silence. It had cost him a lot of money. It was why he'd bought Japanese. They'd engineered the silence in, built the car around it. Had a listening team working with the designers and engineers from day one, just using their ears. The doors closing, the servos in the electric windows, the switches in the dash, the leather, the hushed litany of the powerplant. These were sounds respectful of the silence they inhabited, and served in some way to define it. What all this meant, ultimately, was that Leverton could hear the faint embryonic pulse of an idea behind the rush of his thoughts. See through the glitter of the surface to where the big dark fish rolled. The big, beautiful ideas that his clients paid big, beautiful money for. The money that paid for the car and the house. And the quiet. The big, beautiful quiet.

Ken Leverton woke at six without an alarm, habitually, in the cool of his woodframe house out at Palos Verdes. Showered, took the first of his two daily shaves. Shaved with a blade, as the fretful insect buzz of an electric razor bothered him. Exercised naked in front of the full-height mirrors on the closet doors, measuring his breathing against the tensions in his body. Sleep often left him ricked out of shape, stiff as sticks, and the exercises were for realignment rather than muscle building. Still, he thought, recognizing the insidiously

1

familiar whisper of self-flattery, not bad for an old guy. Normal height, normal build, maybe a little heavy-set. Thick dark hair cut decently short, touch of wave in it. Not handsome, not ugly. Normal guy. He slid into the cool of his judo robe and opened the deck doors, airlock suck and kiss of the rubber seal letting in a warm wave of morning heat. He looked at the palms above the low red roofs across the street, decals laminated on the bright opal panel of the sky. Closed his eyes, watched negative mercury trees sliding over the pulsing blood-black of his eyelids, breathed in the blue air off the ocean. And the sounds; crystalline, echoless, desiccated by sunlight. Tibetan bicycle bell, kid's cartoon laugh, furry ripple of exhaust.

From here he could just see the tiny figures of the whale-watchers down the hill at Point Vicente, climbing into their high canvas chairs for the long day ahead. Save a chair for me, guys, he thought. I'll be needing it any day. Name stitched on the back, notebook, binoculars, faulty prostate. Inevitable.

Little rituals. Spiraling his mantra off into silence. Buttered multigrain toast, lowfat milk so cold it made the glass sweat. In the living room, he unhooked his guitar from the wall. He'd sold the amplifier a lifetime ago, but kept the guitar. It held certain resonances he treasured, embedded into the wood and wire. And he liked its unamplified tone – barely audible, even in the silent room. He stroked the ball of his thumb over the strings, improvising on a mood set by his dreams. He no longer punished himself into remembering his dreams upon waking, no longer probed the turbid entrails for portents. There'd been too many bloody, blind, suffering monsters he knew to be his own dreadful babies. So this little ritual. Some kind of cleansing. This was when he might hear the last murmurs from the cave of sleep, the muddy mutter that had held his head in dream. Occasionally, in a sudden, quietly savage atonality, he could still feel the monsters roil. More often these days (these years), the mood had been meditative, simple, clear as a glass bell. This morning, some trailing thread of doubt had compromised the strength of every major chord with a slide into the lingering uncertainty of its major seventh. This subtly melancholic shift, did it augur anything? He let the final chord fade, unresolved, until he could hear the silence behind it, until he knew he could lift his fingers from the fretboard without killing the vibrations in the strings. He held the guitar up to the wall bracket, a gentle offering, and the small, vertical crease between his eyebrows deepened.

Little rituals in his clear white house. No radio, no TV. Rush sandals on sanded boatdeck floor, white tile. White canvas couch, director chairs. White walls. One closed white door with the handle removed. Passing it without a look, without a thought, same as every morning. Control. Triple-glazed windows and curling black Spanish wrought-iron bars. A raku bowl filled with knotted grass stems. A small Paul Klee drawing – spidery birdman in a twisted wire house – in a zinc frame. Aircon rendered noiseless after they'd replaced it twice. Noiseless, it had said, Leverton pointing to the word in the brochure. Noiseless or your money back. He didn't care about the money. He had money. He wanted no noise. He wanted cool and quiet, while the hot world whirled around him. This simplicity of order, this quiet, this white haven, all this had taken more work than he liked to think about, and more time than he cared to admit.

Dressed in a collarless shirt, buttoned at the neck, an undyed linen suit and black canvas Charles Jordan shoes with no socks, he drove his Zen rock garden car up the coast to Marina Del Rey before cutting across to the office at Century City. It took longer than using the freeway most days, but he liked the calm along the coast, the view of the ocean. He drove slowly, hands resting lightly on the wheel. Liver spots on the tanned backs of his hands. Evidence of the years. Changing his grip, he took a right at the red light, a bum in rags mouthing something terrible at him from the curb, mouth like a slash in a cinema seat. Something inaudible.

I'm Outstanding

Maitland Leverton Associates Corporate Communications took the twenty-third floor of the copper-glazed SS&T tower at Century City. The partners had widescreen ocean-view offices, the designers and writers shared an open-plan bullpen in the center, and the account executives occupied a long room on the other side, looking into the prismatic perspectives of Century City. Leverton always got there early, before anyone else, unless the creatives had been working through the night. As they had this morning. Amity leaned on the laserprinter, examining a shiny print tonguing into the tray.

—Hey, Amy. Any midnight oil left?

She stretched, rolling her head on her neck, the hem of her surf top rising to show a silver ring piercing her belly-button.

—Just burned the last drop on TasteLicious, she said. A pig to get right, for some reason. She took Leverton's wrist in her hand and looked at his watch. Be slapped up for nine-thirty, no problem.

—Get you a coffee?

—Thanks, Ken, she said, sniffing at her underarm. I think I'll take a shower and get changed. Kinda skunky.

Leverton watched her gather the prints and walk away

between the partitions, an unstudied little girl's walk, all slouch and scuff, the backs of her vintage sneakers sawn away so she could slip them on without bothering with the laces. He walked to his office and pressed the code on the door lock and went inside. The sea-colored blinds glowed like yacht sails in a flat calm, filling the room with shadowless pacific light. On his left, Fiona Cavaunagh's desk, with its integral computer workstation and frosted green vase with tiny white flowers she replaced every day. Polished wood-block floor, painted ash furniture. Neutral grasscloth walls, no pictures, no prizes, no patterns. Each of the partner's offices had a circular elemental feature. Leverton had for many years a Zen stone garden, raked gravel around a couple of rocks, but he got tired of the lifelessness, so changed it for a pool with a low slate surround, where two skeleton carp conspired below ace-of-spades leaves, mute as memory. Invariably, they hung at right angles, so he'd given them street names. Sutter and Van Ness. Partners in a detective agency on stake-out, watching, witnessing.

Leverton did very little actual work here. In fact, he did very little actual work. This management stuff, conversations, meetings, just being there, doing a little bit of creative direction, this wasn't work. Amity worked. Like he'd worked a long time ago. So his long table at the window was entirely clear, or should have been. Pale-blue file card placed dead center. It had been the first thing he saw on entering. He ignored it while he raised the blinds and squinted at the sparking wire of the ocean, burned brown by smog to the south, way out over the powder-gray quartz grid of LA. He looked down at the cars beading the thread of Beverly Glen Boulevard, cocktail colors snuffed out by the shadow of the tower. Blue file card.

The elevator doors opened down the hallway, and he heard Peter Reitz's voice buoyed up by a woman's laugh. Yok it up, Peter. He took a heavy aluminum shaker from a drawer and fed the fish, dimpling the skin of the water. Their feeding mouths wattled the featureless reflection of his head. Blue file card. He went to his faded leather chair, replaced the shaker, unfolded his old man's eyeglasses from his jacket pocket, picked up the card.

It wasn't just that he didn't know who'd left the note that bothered him. It was the fact that it was handwritten. Sharp pencil, all caps. He couldn't remember the last time he'd seen anything handwritten. He wondered what his own handwriting looked like, if it had withered and died, untended, a parched vine crabbed against a wall. He didn't even own a pencil, now he came to think of it. Blue file card, five by three. They didn't use them. Paperless office, made a point of it. No memos, no minutes, no notes.

CALL AMBIENT PARAMETERS

And a 310 LA number. What the hell was this? Who the hell was this?

He had thirty minutes before the big swinging dicks from TasteLicious foamed up for the presentation. He flexed the card between his fingers, slid open the telephone drawer and dialed, raising his chin a little so he could see the numbers through his graduated bifocals.

—*Ampar* . . .

What? He could hear one of those pingy digital music chips, like you get in greetings cards. He knew this tune. The theme from that TV show with Elizabeth Montgomery. *Bewitched*. The hell with this. He put the phone down.

7

—Line lost.

Huh? He frowned at the telephone, set in its custom-made drawer. Thinking the connection was still open, he picked it up, heard the soft burr of the dead line. He replaced it carefully, feeling the click under the handset.

—Up down up down.

He grinned up at Fiona Cavaunagh, dropping her purse on her desk.

—Hey, Fee. Listen, could you check out my phone? It's talking to itself.

—Hi, Ken, she said, dabbing at the corner of her eye with a Kleenex. Talking to itself. Sure, I'll get right onto it. Her own phone flashed. She sat on the edge of her desk and took the call, hooking her blond hair away from her ear. Morning, Brian, she said, rolling her eyes at Leverton. Her daily hot-ear session with Brian Mulready, their guy in NY. Might as well be their guy in her lap for all the time he spends on the phone, Leverton thought. He watched Fiona replace the flowers, cradling the phone between her chin and shoulder, crossing her legs, saying Okay, and Sure, no problem.

Kirby Klein put her head around the door, her copper bob swinging in a bright blade.

—Ken? You want to give the TasteLicious thing a quick pre?

—Surely. It'll have to be quick, too. Uh, Fee, we're in the Green Room?

He joined Klein in the bullpen. She was wearing a tight little charcoal suit over a dull black silk shirt with a pewter clip at the neck, black stockings, patent pumps. He always thought of her as taller somehow, maybe because she was so beautifully proportioned, and surprised himself again by how short she was standing next to him.

8

—Achingly fabulous ensemble, he said. Have I seen this little combo before?

—Little? she said sharply, not letting the patronizing adjective go by. It's Donna, she said, grabbing a cup at the watercooler. And I didn't pay retail.

—*That's five.*

—I'm sorry? Leverton said, turning to see where the voice came from, seeing nobody.

—I didn't pay retail, she repeated, dropping the empty cup in the recycling bag. You okay, Ken?

—Yeah, he said, rubbing his jaw. Satellite delay. He opened the Green Room door for her. Framed awards on the walls, non-hierarchical ameboid table, bottle-green Thai silk wallcovering, seamless white curved presentation wall at the end. Amity and a guy from the art room rushed by behind them and Klein said, Twenty minutes. Yo, they said, tripping over each other.

—Pre me up, Kirb, Leverton said. If I can look as though I know why I'm here it may be a plus.

Klein leaned on the table, touching her fingernails on the blond wood. Predatory. Her eyes, heavy-lidded, met his as she talked.

—Essentially, she said, they're scared shitless. They come on like corporate hard-ons, but it's all flounce. They've been with Wendell's since Martin was with Lewis, and everybody's tired. They want to move but they don't want to move. So we have two routes. More of the same, but different. Or different, but more of the same. I'm taking neither. It's worse than they think, and I'm going to rub their face in it.

Leverton smiled opaquely, said nothing. This means nothing to me, he thought. Then, at the same time, they both turned and saw Curtis Maitland in the doorway. He had that power over them still. The ability to magnetize attention, quick as a trick. After all these years, he could still do it. It was what made MLA different, and the clients knew it. Take him away and you've got yourself just another hot-shop full of great teeth and ponytails and pushy guys with Prozac wives. Something to do with the stature of the guy, for sure, the height, the strength in the stance, but more to it than that. He had the bearing and the confidence of the handsome, and gave the impression of being good-looking in a severe way, but his face was a little too planar to be beautiful, his broken nose set too harshly, his eyes set too deep. Yet he was thought of as handsome. There was an intensity, almost a density about him, a bright mineral quality to his pale gray eyes and an edge to his voice that expressed a clarity, an authority, a total lack of doubt that seduced and convinced immediately. When you thought of Curtis Mait-land you remembered the shape — the profile, perhaps, or the silhouette he cut in a doorway — as a sequence of almost monolithic images, not as a moving thing at all. Like a series of shapes printed on cards, which when fanned by the thumb give the illusion of animation, each shape was a character in his own private alphabet. He moved from pose to pose — from letter to letter — but the pose was the man, not affectation. Soberly suited, his evenly graying hair just curled over the collar to his button-down Oxford-cloth shirt. His club tie had a full Windsor knot, and his black brogues gleamed like licked licorice. Leverton always felt rumpled when Maitland was in the room. He pushed a hand through his own hair uselessly, apologetically, unconsciously. Mait-land grinned.

—Good morning, Kirby, Ken. Any incompletions?

—Kirby was just giving me a quick pre. It sounds simple enough, but then I didn't understand what she was saying.

—All you need know, dear, she said, putting a hand on his arm and mouthing the words very clearly, is that Taste-Licious will sweat dollars like rain with Kirby's tiny hand on the thermostat.

Maitland chuckled, showing his absurdly perfect teeth. Let's not worry about the side-effects, he said.

—At least, Leverton said, let's not kid ourselves. I'm just here to take the coats.

Klein and Maitland exchanged looks during a short silence. Your perspective is always valued, Ken, said Maitland. Always will be.

Yeah, thought Leverton. A perspective that's getting closer to falling out the picture all the time.

Peter Reitz, the young pretender with the floppy center-part, put his head round the door and said, They're up. Leverton had caught him sitting in his chair one time, trying it for size. Reitz had recovered from his embarrassment too quickly for Leverton's liking, and now met his eye easily, with a knowing edge that could have been insulting. Hell, thought Leverton, he could have the chair, the car slot in the shade, the clients that ate Tokyo, the thirty-three and a third percent of their debt. Reitz was hungry enough to take them on, and he was good. But he couldn't have it all yet. Leverton was waiting for the moment. The moment when he'd know he didn't belong here anymore; when the whale-watchers at Point Vicente turned in their canvas chairs and beckoned him over, calling his name. Until then, the guy could sweat it a little. Reitz disappeared, Klein and Maitland exchanging a few quiet words.

Watching them, Leverton felt suddenly old and out of it.

11

He only had eight years on Maitland, but eighteen on Klein, and they hurt. It wasn't just a matter of energy. He was fitter than he'd been since college. It wasn't the technology leaving him behind, either. He hadn't been hands-on since they'd bought out Derndale's and wired in their people a decade ago. And it wasn't midlife crisis. He'd swerved through that too drunk even to pronounce male menopause. So why did he now feel like he was dead, a shadow on a shade, when he looked at Kirby Klein? Maitland had asked, a little predictably, if there were any incompletions. Looking now at Kirby Klein, catching her beautiful sad eyes just as they slid away, Leverton could only think of one.

He tried to key himself out of this major-seventh mood while Reitz ushered in the six suits from TasteLicious, made the introductions. Regulation corporate preeners with the don't-fuck-with-the-money vibe. He forgot all their names right away, even the brittle little token woman with the bizarrely Nashville hair and munchkins-who-lunch suit. He found a seat at the back, watching how Klein effortlessly froze the woman out, moving amongst the others like a cool breeze on a hot day, preparing their soft pulpy underparts for the rusty machete. Even Maitland powered down the personality to give her the spot, standing in a corner, unblinking, intent, hands lightly clasped at crotch level.

—Gentlemen, she said when they were all seated, and Leverton, watching the Hair Woman closely, saw her eyelid flicker. Gentlemen, Klein repeated, you have a problem.

She thumbed a remote, dimming the lights, and an image flashed on the panoramic wall behind her, back-projected from the next room. It was an image familiar to TasteLicious, and to many Americans. A coarsegrained newspaper shot of a dirty bum on a dirty toilet floor, a dirty needle in his dirty arm. Leverton sensed a quickening of the corporate pulse, a tightening of the corporate sphincter. Go for 'em, Kirb, he thought.

—You know what this is? Klein said, looking round at the ugly image. Sure they knew, thought Leverton. This was Bradley Brewster, the TasteLicious Tyke, dead at forty-eight, a bag of dirty scag. The nation's favorite breakfast-food kid, whose cheery cowboy-hatted head had adorned the packet for nearly forty years. Had his own TV show, too, before his career flatlined into premature teen obscurity and class-A pharmacy. Technically, cause of death wasn't clear; a combination of cardiac arrest following a heroin overdose, lungs covered in fur from an AIDS-related illness, and a bad and savage beating that left him lying in a hot swamp of blood and shit in the toilets of the Latimer Hotel. One way or another, his card had been marked. For almost an entire day his death had filled the attention span of the nation. A couple of handwringing think-pieces in the weeklies had seized upon his squalid demise as a paradigm of the loss of innocence in America. How could this happen? Are we all guilty?

—I think, someone said dryly, that we're all only too familiar with who this is. This is three weeks ago, Ms Klein. It's old news.

Leverton saw Hair Woman allow herself a thin smile.

—Not who this is, Klein interrupted, spreading a hand on the table, crimson nails drumming the wood. *What* this is. Anybody?

Klein milked the silence for exactly the right amount of time. This, gentlemen, is a teeshirt. It's their bestselling line. She thumbed the remote again, and the picture widened to show the image silk-screened onto the front of a shortsleeve tee, with the familiar copyrighted phrase '*Gee Moms, it's TasteLicious!*' in corporate typestyle above. Leverton heard the breathing stop. Somebody actually said *Shit* under their breath.

—And this is yesterday, Mr Petersen. Peter Reitz passed her a copy of *Rolling Stone* magazine and she flung it onto the table, open at the classifieds. Another click on the remote threw up images of the magazine cover and the ad to either side of Bradley Brewster. It was a wonderful, wonderful moment, and Leverton felt like hugging her. Naked, from behind.

—They're dead, said a suit, pushing away the magazine. They're dead.

—With respect, Klein said, our concern is not to put a teeshirt company out of business, but to get the nation's premier quality breakfast product back into the American heart. Because it is there – its home in the consumer heartlands – that its presence has become diminished . . .

Und so weiter. Leverton wiped a grin off his face with his hand. They were mush. They were day-old breakfast cereal, and the account was already portfolioed. Klein piled it on, beating them up with their own sales figures, building to the point when she snapped her fingers for the blinds to come down for the creative presentation. At that moment, during that precisely engineered silence, so full of anticipation, Leverton heard a loud voice behind him say *Hot hot hot*.

He laughed encouragingly, craning his head around, wondering who was getting off on the presentation. He found himself staring at the airconditioner grille in the wall. The laughter died in his throat. He turned back to a few bemused glances, but Klein recovered quickly, flashing up the first slide. Leverton covered the bottom half of his face with his hand, kept his goddamn mouth shut for the next eighty minutes.

Klein's presentation left TasteLicious gratifyingly humbled and enthusiastic. There was an air of exhaustion and relief. She'd rubbed their Ivy League noses in some pretty grubby facts, and then shown them how MLA was going to address the problems within the culture of the organization, author a process of cultural change, and express that change through authentic strategy. That was the fun part. Austin, their Creative Director, and Amity dazzled them with color, like dangling beads and mirrors. Afterward, Klein slid up to Leverton, folded into his chair like someone in a rest home. She leaned to whisper in his ear.

—Ken, why don't you slip down the laundry chute on this one? We're only going to burp them and show them the animals.

Leverton unfolded his legs, felt a knee pop. Yeah, he said. Sorry about the miscued canned laughter back there. Bit distracted this morning for some reason.

—It's unlike you. I'm concerned. Anything you want to talk about? Can I watch you eat lunch?

—That would be fine. Le Park? Around one?

—Ish?

—Great, he said. Thanks, Kirb. She was already gone, introducing somebody to Maitland. He slipped back to his office, tried to concentrate on Fee's messages, looking at the blank expanse of his desk.

—Uh, Fee, that note on my table . . .

She frowned. Note? I'm sorry?

—On my table first thing. Blue file card. Have you moved it?

She pursed her lips in thought. Sorry, Ken, you got me. I haven't seen any cards.

—Okay, not important. Listen, do we know people called Ambient something-or-other, Parameters?

She frowned harder, clacked at her keyboard, repeating the syllables of the name. Not on the database, she said. Supplier or client?

—Beats me. Doesn't matter. I'm going for lunch.

—You have Tara Van Zandt at two.

Leverton knocked his forehead with the heel of his hand.

—Jesus. Tara Van Zandt. Tara Van Zandt. He went to his desk, moved around it, looking on the floor, opening drawers. You sure you didn't see the note?

Fee's phone flashed. She picked it up, grateful for the distraction.

Kirby Klein collapsed back in her chair, flipped her patent pumps off her feet, sending them clattering onto the woodblock floor.

—Like me a little?

They were alone in her office. She watched Maitland brush a fingertip through the waist-high savannah grass growing in the planter that formed her office's elemental feature. She had deliberately put the subject on a personal level, as if she'd taken on the project to petition for acceptance. Maitland was never personal, always made the step from the context of expressed personality to the context of the conversation. His use of language was intimidating at first, then hard work, then frequently a bore. Then you found yourself using it too. First time she'd tried to do the same trick, back when she'd been in awe of him, maybe a little in love. Wasn't her style, and they both knew it. And

16

they both knew she never did anything to be liked. His reply, when it came, was measured and anticipated. She awarded herself bonus points for predicting his first phrase word for word.

—They were listening for the missings. Your stance was uncompromising, but entirely appropriate. I thought we had completion in there. There's a context for action that wasn't there before. Did you get that?

Klein pushed her fingers back through her hair, tilting her chin up to show her long neck, feeling her brassiere lift her breasts. She sighed, enjoying the moment. It had been a tough one to pull in. She'd patiently warmed up her own cold call of six months back, working her way into their confidence. MLA usually picked up new clients through referrals, and very occasionally Brian Mulready beat a door down with his fist. On the TasteLicious offensive, Maitland had not been as supportive as he could, keeping his distance. At one point he'd been actively discouraging. They make breakfast cereal, he'd said. Are we sure they're the right profile for our portfolio? Klein wondered if he found the process a little vulgar, somehow. Or maybe he was getting lazy, didn't like the hunt anymore. Whatever. She knew the money, at least, would have exactly the right profile for the portfolio.

—The earth moved for me, she said. But Ken – did you notice? I mean, of course you noticed. You notice an eyelash out of place. I'm worried about the guy.

Maitland sat on the edge of her desk, hitching his pants leg so it didn't bag at the knee. Klein saw the sheen of silk sock at his ankle, wondered if he still wore the silk boxers she'd gifted him back when . . .

—Your concern is appropriate. His focus was disengaged,

17

and it may be a pointer for us. We've never talked about Ken, have we? It's a missing for us. Want to create a safe space?

Klein knew this technique. Non-judgmental listening. No right/wrong binds. Say what you are. First time, the safe space had finished up in his bed. They'd had completion on that one, at least. It had been surprisingly civilized, his reaction to her not wanting to take it any further. To do it again. After the second time. It had taken them both by surprise when it happened, and it had never been mentioned since by either of them. But it had been good. And there were times when she . . .

—It's a hard time for Ken, she said. He can't let go. I know he's working this up into a real big thing, and he needn't. He started the whole retirement issue himself, remember. Too old, out of touch, stale, all that. We weren't saying that. We've never said that.

Maitland's voice was soft, reassuring. So what's possible here? What are we looking at? What's the possibility for action? What's the context?

She sighed. This was work. Everything reduced to content and context, possibilities for action. Sometimes she got something out of the process, sometimes just a headache. One more time.

—The context is Ken's contribution to the whole, she said. The content is the bind he's in. The possibilities are a) he fucks up and we bag him up, or, b) he shifts his own context of what he can contribute. Change the paradigm. And I don't know how he'd do that, but the perspective you mentioned earlier may be an appropriate model. Broaden it, narrow it, I don't know, but start it from a different point.

18

The effort of talking like this got to her suddenly. She stared at him.

—Can we cut the overheated dialog? Ken's problem, however he sees it, is ours too. It's true, though, isn't it? I just don't want him to screw anything up. Like, name the day, Ken.

Maitland checked a cufflink, said nothing. Klein said, I really don't want to patronize him by feeling sorry for him. But I do. I mean, the guy is basically a lonely man. Who's he got except us?

—With Ken, Maitland said, there's always a woman. Your sympathy is a little misconceived. His big picture is the one we all work within. Wherever his perspective is coming from, it's always valued.

Klein sensed that this wasn't all he had to say. She could see, unusually, a little uncertainty in his expression. He hadn't practiced this, didn't know the words. She waited.

—Ken has a complex history with me, he said. It hasn't been easy for him. You didn't know him when we started. I don't think it's ever been easy for him. What you see is what he's learned to do, and it's been a hard lesson for him. You see a successful, respected, creative guy who's got life totally wrapped.

Klein was uncertain if the pause was hers to fill. Maitland saved her the trouble. He looked at her when he spoke, and, as usual, she found the intensity unsettling, narrowed her eyes and tilted her head slightly to cope with it.

—It's not exactly a secret that he's an alcoholic, he said. He doesn't drink, but he's still an alcoholic. That's the context for what he does – illness. The fact that he's made all the possibilities for action within that context is really heroic.

19

But I never forget that is his context. And his behavior today was expressive of that context. Totally authentic. I have been aware of an ongoing retraction in his commitment for some time. It is a concern.

Klein looked at her shoes, tipped up against the side of the planter. She'd known Leverton to be an alcoholic, although they'd never talked about it. Maybe he'd been drinking again. Or the urge to drink was distractingly strong. The fear of it. Maybe retirement was a big hole he'd fill with drink.

—Your thoughts? said Maitland.

—His problem is our problem, she said. And it must stop before it gets to the clients. We should extend this safe space to include him. I can't think of formulating some kind of solution without him.

Maitland stood up, glanced discreetly at his watch, worn on the inside of his wrist. I have to go.

—Me too, she said. I'm chowing down with him at Le Park. Maybe I can cheer the guy up a little.

—Have the turbot, Maitland said over his shoulder. That would cheer up eastern Europe. Outstanding.

Klein watched him move his shoulders as he adjusted his tie on the way out. No, she thought, outstanding is landing a major account from a cold call. I'm outstanding.

Nothing But Fear

She found Leverton sitting at his usual table up on the half-mezzanine, hidden by hanging plants from the noisy checkered floor of the restaurant, where media mavens gathered to talk to people they weren't with and laugh that half-beat too long. She glanced around for Dean Mance. Her husband would cameo through Le Park on a regular basis, talking up some movie deal, fielding calls on his cellphone. She didn't see him today, which made things simpler. Leverton got up to greet her and moved an upholstered aluminum garden chair for her.

—Kirb. You eating?

—Maybe, she said as she sat down. He looked preoccupied, not meeting her eye. He poured her a glass of water.

—Great show this morning, he said.

—Thanks. I was kind of on my own back there.

—Yeah. Sorry about that.

She gave him a look. Oh, it's not you I'm talking about. I may need you later. I just missed some support at the sharp end, that's all. You know.

—I thought Curtis was giving you your space?

—I got agoraphobia with the space Curtis gave me on this one. Still, no matter. Old Kirby reeled this one in by herself, didn't she?

—I'm proud for you, Kirb. Really I am. Want to celebrate with a five-leaf salad?

She shook her head. Ken, we have to talk, you and me. We really do.

He picked up a fork and balanced it in his fingers. Okay, he said.

—You're not on the button this morning, Ken. Not like you.

He invented a smile. Ah, he said. You noticed, huh? I thought I finessed through on that one.

—Where are you, Ken? I mean, phone home . . .

He breathed out through his nose, letting his shoulders slump. It's just this, I don't know, this whole . . .

—Say it, she whispered, wide-eyed, separating the syllables. Say the big bad word.

—Retirement, he said, in a tone of embarrassed confession. This whole retirement thing. Getting to me, I guess.

She looked at him. Five years' professional relationship with the guy, you'd think they talked. She realized how very little she knew about him. More than that, she was surprised how much she wanted to know. He was staring at the fork in his fingertips.

—*Stab*.

He dropped the fork like it was red hot, knocked over a glass. The fork spun and rang on the tiled floor. He watched it, horrified, as Klein watched him. Neither spoke. A waiter came by, swept it up, stood by their table, smiling.

—Are you ready to order or should I let you ponder a little longer?

Klein broke the silence with difficulty, transfixed by Leverton's blue staring eyes, frozen open mouth. Oh, we're pondering, she said. Thank you, Steven.

22

—No problem. The waiter righted the glass, filled it from a bottle, and retreated into the foliage.

—Wow, Ken, she said. You're really stressed up about this.

She reached a hand toward him across the table instinctively. Leverton went to hold it, held back. Did you hear it? he said. Of course you didn't. Jesus, Kirb. I'm sorry. /

—Hear what?

He touched her hand, avoiding her eye. Nothing. I'm okay. I just need some time off, I guess.

—That's what retirement is, Ken. I wish I could retire, I really do.

Leverton put a fist to his mouth, knuckled an incisor. No, you don't, Kirb. Retired guys, I see them every day, waiting for the whales at Point Vicente. They line up the same every day, with their parasols and their binoculars and their diaries. Stitch their names on the backs of their chairs.

Klein's face wrinkled in puzzlement. What? Whale-watchers? I don't get it.

—It's like they're waiting for me. They're happy, they're good people, and they scare me to death.

Klein laughed, a soft, low laugh full of affection. You don't have to watch the whales if you don't want to, stupid. Kirby promises.

—What else is there? Spend time with the family? I haven't heard from my wife in twenty years. Got no kids, no grandchildren, no family to hang around and delight with my backwoods wisdom and pipe-whittling.

—Curtis doesn't want you to clear your desk, Ken, nobody does. Why not just wind down a little, say put in a couple days a week? It's like you're pulling yourself out by

23

the roots. Scale it down. Either that, or, you know, name the day, get over it. Visit Europe. Write your book.

—Watch the fucking whales.

Klein watched his face harden, his eyes narrow. I can't help you like this, Ken. Listen, you're, what, fifty-five?

—Yeah. No. Fifty-six.

—Whatever. CEOs rputinely stumble into the office into their seventies for directorial duties. You're the same age as Mick Jagger. You're not ready to watch whales full-time. You're too damn young and frisky. And you got another ten good years before you get to beige out.

—Beige out?

—Sure. That time in your life when all the color drains out of it. Happened to my folks last fall, virtually overnight. Drop by their apartment and you have trouble seeing them against the wallpaper. I have to use my hands to find them. Look at you. You're a big, sexy guy, Ken. You got more hair than seems exactly right, you own your own house and your own teeth, and you apparently get more dates than a calendar factory. You got, who knows? Thirty more years? More? Three fabulous fun-filled decades. It's what you work for. What's the problem?

Leverton smiled at her. There'd been times in the last five years when he'd had to bite his lip when the urge to bite hers became too strong. He'd got that down to about once a day. Twice, tops. Kirby Klein was struggling to make a second marriage work and Leverton hadn't wanted to complicate things for her, or compromise their working relationship, the best and most creative he'd ever had. And he was old enough to be, well, older. Old enough to be too old.

—There's a whole bunch of stuff I have to deal with right now, he said. I don't want to turn this into the Ken Leverton

24

Cozy Club, but how much do you think you know about me?

Klein shrugged, pinched her finger and thumb together. Half this?

—Right, he said. So I don't know where to start.

—How about this morning, by the watercooler? That's when you went AWOL on me all of a sudden.

—We have to spool back a bit on this one. Got the time for a misty-eyed trip down memory lane?

Klein nodded, without checking her watch. Sure.

—Okay, he continued. Maybe a year or so after Curtis and me got started, this would be in 'seventy-five, 'seventy-six, my wife walks. Because of my working, because of my drinking, because of me, whatever. I couldn't blame her. I was too drunk to even see her leave. So I seal her room up and drink her out of my head. I'm out of the loop for three years, fucking up all over. Curtis, God bless him, hides me from the clients, hides me from everybody, keeps me alive and on the payroll. Three years when I'm hearing voices in my head on a twenty-four-hour basis. The thing with voices in your head, see, is that they're much clearer, like a direct-to-cortex input of pure sound. They're really in there.

His voice tailed off into silence. Klein waited, unwilling to break the spell. What had he heard that she hadn't? When he picked up the thread again, he was looking down at her hand, turning her wedding band with his thumb, without really being aware of what he was doing.

—Ever since Curtis dragged me through my three-year weekend, I've been listening to the silence in my head. Not only listening to it, but listening for it. I need to know it's there. My life revolves around order and calm and quiet. This is an order I find increasingly difficult to maintain.

25

Work is more and more of a distraction for me. I'm simply not involved in it enough to control it.

He poured some water with his free hand. Couple months back, he said, I was at the heart of it, or I thought I was. Now I'm told my perspective is valuable. That really sums it up. My perspective? I only have that perspective as a function of distance. I'm staring out of the window. I'm ducking meetings. Tara Van Zandt. She's getting pissed at me, and that's dangerous. Clients get pissed at me, word gets around. I can't hang around pissing people off. Can't wait until you and Curtis have to tell me to bag my stuff up, that'll be too late. Maybe retirement is the wrong word. Maybe what I'm trying to do is quit. Just quit.

Klein thought about what he'd said for a minute. He was still turning her wedding band.

—You said there was a bunch of stuff you were worrying about.

Leverton looked up. You don't want to know, he said. Believe me. You are not in a need-to-know situation.

Klein wasn't taking this. I do need to know, she said. Your problem is our problem. If you're . . . ill, you must share it with us.

She regretted the word as soon as she said it.

—Ill? I'm not ill, Kirb. Fit as a butcher's dog. So you can quit worrying about that. It's just delayed menopause. Or adolescence. Or advancing senility. Whatever. I'll be okay. I'll sort it out. I've got it under control.

Steven came by and they made their choices, and spent the rest of the meal talking about Bradley Brewster and the death of the American Dream. Klein kept her eye on Leverton all the while, when she wasn't looking for her husband. If something else was going on in his head, he kept

26

it covered up. But it was the hint of control in the technique of his charm, which he usually exercised effortlessly, that ultimately gave him away. That tiny bit more distance between them. It is the attempt to control, she thought, that brings the shutters rattling down, and the desire to control is born of nothing but fear.

I'm Happy

Tara Van Zandt sat in the Green Room, her legs crossed, tapping a flesh-shiny fingernail on her watch crystal. Amity was shuffling through a few preliminary concepts, fanning out the roughs on the table, overcompensating for the zero input of her boss. Van Zandt looked up without changing position, saw Leverton gazing out the window.

—So, she said, in the same conversational key she'd been using with Amity. The lifestyle approach. What's your view, Ken?

Leverton just sat there, the muscles working in his face like a dog moving in its sleep. Van Zandt's voice was soft, but her eyes were like dirty ice. You think I should just walk the hell out of here and take the account with me.

Amity, horrified, could hear Leverton's teeth grind together through his clenched jaw. Van Zandt shouldered her briefcase and walked out, her clicking heels taking up the beat of her fingernail against her watch. A frozen moment later, Amity followed her, picking up the concept boards, looking back at Leverton with a face full of baffled anger.

He realized there was a hand on his shoulder. Maybe it had been there for some time. His mouth was dry, tongue felt like a coral shelf ornament. His jaw ached.

—Go home, Ken, said Maitland softly. Take the rest of the day off. See how you feel in the morning. Call me.

Leverton turned his head on his stiff neck. Maitland sat on the edge of the table. Amity had her head around the door. It's okay, Amity, Maitland said without turning. Get Tara Van Zandt's mobile for me, would you?

Klein took the call at home that night.

—Kirb? Ken. Sorry to call you at home. I guess Curtis told you about this afternoon.

Klein wrapped the towel around her wet hair with one hand. Yeah, I heard something about that. Where are you?

—I'm at home. I was wondering . . . Can we meet?

The pause was too short to notice, but she did a lot of thinking in it before she spoke. Sure, she said. Want me to swing by? Did you eat yet?

She heard him sigh. No, he said. Lost my appetite today.

—Listen, I'll be there in thirty, okay? You don't eat, you die.

She collapsed the antenna on the handset by stabbing the pillow with it. Shit, she said, the word a cut-off jet of steam. She rubbed her hair dry and buttoned the fly of her Levi's.

—Dean? she said, and again, a little louder. Dean?

She pushed her feet into deck shoes, pulled a tee over her head, and went into the living room. Dean Mance was on the balcony, listening to his cellphone, frowning darkly, pinching the bridge of his nose. Klein made a goofy wave to get his attention. He flapped an irritable hand at her and turned his back. This was the quality time they'd promised themselves, of course. Real prime-time relationship-building. Dean making a big career sacrifice by coming home in daylight. Pacing the balcony in his baggy Italian shirt, fielding

29

calls. Turning his back on her. The fuck. She took a kitchen spatula and wrote BYE DEAR in moussaka on the glass screen between the kitchen and the living room, taking care to get the letters in reverse so he could read it. She scooped up the keys to the Porsche and left without shutting the door.

—This isn't causing problems for you and Dean? Leverton said. He was wearing his work clothes and fooling with the blind cord by the window, feeling as crumpled as he looked. Klein stood in the open doorway, hand on her hip.

—Oh right, she said heavily. Dean couldn't break a call if I fucked him with a hot lava lamp. I swear, Ken, I called him on our own balcony last night. From the kitchen. Took the phone off the wall and got him between deals. He didn't think it was funny.

—I think it's funny.

Klein narrowed an eye at him, thinking, What is going on in there? Maybe, she said, I'll call you next time. You can come and eat his dinner while we watch him push his hand through his hair on the balcony.

—*twirrrrl*

She saw his eye twitch, like a flinch, like a fly in his eye. She said, You're not really very okay, are you?

He rubbed his face with his hand, pulling his cheeks back into a grin. Sure, he said. No, not really, I guess. Yeah, I'm okay. I'd just really appreciate some, ah, human conversation right now. Don't want to be on my own tonight. This evening. Really appreciate it, Kirby. Way things are going, today could be my last day at the office.

—That bad, huh? Well, don't lose any sleep over Dean. I left him his dinner. Where we going for ours?

—I can fix us something here.

30

—Like a blade of dry grass and a pebble in a plate of steam, maybe? Sorry, Ken, I got a major carbo jones. This is nice, though, your place. Been how long since I was here?

—The Dietmar party. 'Ninety-four? When I still 'entertained'.

—There's something different. You done something?

—Bagged the party snacks last Tuesday.

—That'd be it, then. Oh, and I'm driving. No, really, shut up here, Ken. You're hearing voices in your head. I'm driving, okay?

Leverton watched Klein at the wheel of the Porsche, the lights on Sepulveda crawling around her sunglasses, snaking along the tortoiseshell plastic into her hair. The lights were there in her hair, too, little pulses of colored copper. She always wore sunglasses driving. She'd told him she wore them in bed, too.

—I didn't say I was hearing voices in my head, he said evenly.

Klein looked at him, and he saw her eyebrows appear above the rim of her sunglasses. Right, she said, and stiffened her leg against the brake pedal. The Porsche slewed to halt, cars swerving to either side, horns mewling. Klein, lurching back in her seat, grabbed a cigarette from a pack on the dash.

—Got a light?

Leverton, gasping, loosened the grip of the seatbelt across his chest.

—Jesus, Kirby, you'll get us killed . . . Pull over, for Christ's sake . . .

—It'll take more than one passive Camel to kill you, Ken, trust me.

—Okay, okay. Pull over. Really.

—You'll stop dicking me around?

Somebody was blocked in behind them, flashing head-lights, hammering the horn.

—I already stopped. You haven't noticed?

Klein put the car into gear and crept up to forty miles an hour before pulling over and lighting her cigarette. Leverton unclipped his seatbelt and pulled his shirt free of his chest. Know what kind of a guy blows his horn in a situation like that? he said.

—Tell me.

—Guy with a big gun under the seat. Big enough to make him feel really confident it's bigger than the one you may have under yours.

Klein hooked off her shades and leaned across his lap. How convenient, she said, pointing out his window. He looked up out at the mansard-roofed Fatburger concession. Figures moving behind the steamed-up window.

—Couple things I can't understand, Kirb. One: how anybody could get backing for a burger bar franchise called Fatburger. Two: how anybody could possibly expect me to eat there.

—C'mon, cowboy. You can chew my garnish. And that's not an offer I make to every guy.

They found a clear table and Klein put their tray down. There was a bunch of kids with huge inflated jackets and socks on their heads at the next table, grabbing stuff from each other's cartons with their fingers. Klein bit into her half-pound cheeseburger, her nails puncturing the soft bun.

—You're red in tooth and claw, aren't you, Kirb?

—I love meat, she said, her mouth full of it. I'm the last

guy in LA who thinks being at the top of the food chain is a privilege, not a curse. What can I say? More to the point here, what can you say? Eat your salad.

Leverton stirred the salad around with a plastic fork. You want me to eat or talk? he said.

Klein swallowed, chin dipping with the effort. I just thought what was different.

—Huh?

—About your house, remember? You have a guitar on the wall, real noticeable, like a feature? That's new. Breaks up the minimalism.

—I've had that a long time. Always been there.

—Wasn't there for your party.

—Okay. Maybe I took it down. Didn't want people playing it. Leave a guitar around, always some guy wants to do 'Stairway To Heaven'. What are we talking about?

—You're drinking again.

It was Leverton's turn to laugh. He turned the paper cup of Coke in his hand, swirling the ice around. Okay, he said. That's an easy one. I haven't drunk alcohol in any form since I dried out on New Year's Eve in 'seventy-nine. Not a drop.

Klein wiped her mouth with the napkin.

—So where are the voices coming from?

Leverton rolled his eyes. I think I wish I'd never mentioned it. Really.

—*Round we go.*

—What about this afternoon? We may lose a medium-weight client. Amity said it was like you'd gone crazy, like a crazy person. Like you weren't there at all. Just an hour earlier you were fanning me the big breeze about how you could handle it, how in control you were.

Leverton placed the sticky cup on the table and wiped his

fingers on a napkin. He looked around the restaurant. The kids were barking with laughter, thrown back in their seats like crash test dummies.

—It's just that I'm more stressed up than I thought, I guess, he said. Van Zandt will be back. Curtis gave her a call.

Klein stared at him, right in his eyes, her head slightly on one side. He couldn't hold the stare, even through the sunglasses.

—You called me, Ken. So here I am. Watching you eat a salad and lie through your teeth at the same time. This is not a pretty sight.

Leverton went to speak, shut up as Klein continued.

—And we did this stuff once today already. I really want to help, but if you want to be Clint Eastwood, you find someone else to be impressed, okay? I broke into family quality time to be here, too.

Leverton fidgeted in his plastic bucket seat. Kind of hard to talk here, Kirb. Hard to talk anyway, but somewhere quieter, like maybe a south-central crack house during a raid, say, might be more conducive. I'm not dicking you around.

Klein pushed her napkin into her cup.

—Sure. Forgive me. I got the carbos, I'm cool. How about Bobbie's? I could use a good five-cent cigar right now.

Bobbie's was a smoker's club owned by Bobbie Herrera, the go-go dancer at the Cheetah back in the sixties who hung with the Rat Pack until her sinuses collapsed along with her career. There were black-and-white photographs of her and Frank, her in a cage at the Cheetah, her and Dino, her throwing herself across the laps of a bunch of heavy-jawed guys in heavy suits. A signed print of a bare-chested Peter Lawford swinging her into a pool. There was a bar big enough for a string quartet to fight for a place at, and a dim room full of people looking past each other's heads for someone who wasn't there. Low tables with piles of slightly grubby art books for class. Battered leather club chairs.

A guy behind the polished mahogany bar greeted Klein by name, started building her a drink.

—Regular face, huh? said Leverton.

—I'm family. Buy you a drink?

—Hell, yes. Club soda with a lot of attitude.

They found a couch in a dark corner, barricaded by ferns and a Tiffany shade. Klein sipped her daiquiri and set fire to a cigar. Okay, she said, fanning away the smoke. Give.

Leverton rested a foot on the edge of the table. I have heard voices today, sure. But I guess it's some kind of residual chemistry slopping around up there. Maybe because I'm stressed out, my resistance is down, whatever.

She frowned, cigar stopped an inch from her lips. These voices, she said. They're there all the time? Now?

Leverton rubbed his chin, the stubble reminding him he'd missed a shave. Nope, he said. Just intermittent. Isolated. It's not like the full-blown DTs, believe me. I'd have been out the window. That did happen. They wouldn't shut up, I threw myself through a second-floor window. Look . . .

He smoothed his hair back at the temple, bent toward her. She frowned at the pale-gray calligraphy in the tan, like a mark on a map.

—Cicatrice, she said.

—What?

—I always thought that was a much more honorable word than scar. So, it's not enough to send you through the window. Think it'll get that way?

He sighed, sinking back in the couch. I don't know. I

don't think I could go through that again. I really couldn't go through that again, Kirb.

—Anyone you can see? Alcoholics Anonymous?

—I haven't been to a meeting for fifteen years. Last time, I looked around at all the people, thought, They're all alcoholics here. Do I want to spend time with alcoholics? How interesting can that be? If I was drinking again, maybe. Maybe it's nothing to do with drink. That scares me more.

Klein drank some more, sucked at her cigar. What do they say? These voices? What do they sound like?

—I can't remember, to be honest. Just short phrases, words. Meaningless. They sound different. To each other. They're not like anybody I know, if that's what you mean. They're not even talking to me, now I come to think about it. It's like little fragments I'm overhearing. There's none of that horrible gloating accusatory tone of DT voices. It's like moving a dial over a radio station. That's it pretty exactly.

—Can you hear them now?

Leverton shook his head.

—So how did you silence them last time around?

—Pills. Counseling; meditation, but drugs mainly. There's one specifically for voices in the head. A shut-the-fuck-up pill.

—So you can take it again?

—Yeah. Trouble is, it shuts everything else up as well. Turns your head into a Fatburger.

—So, see your doctor. If he thinks you need the pills, see how it goes. Maybe it is just stress, reactivating something in your head, stirring up the sediment. If you're sick, Ken, you have to give work a break. See a shrink. You have no choice. Apart from anything else, we're a partnership.

Leverton nodded slowly. Yep, he said. This much is clear.

—Good. Want to talk about something else for a while?

—God, yes. Anything you like. Never get tired of hearing your voice.

Klein smiled, eyes down. We-ell, she said, I'd kind of like to talk to you about Curtis. There's something been nagging at me about the TasteLicious deal.

—Dumb me up, Kirb.

—Did you watch him during the presentation?

—Can't say I noticed. Backgrounded himself to give you the spot.

—How like him is that, exactly?

Leverton held up a finger and thumb pinched together. Half this much?

Klein laughed briefly, coughing out smoke. Exactly. He powered himself right down to the point of sucking the light in. I had to actually introduce him to the suits afterward. They didn't know him from a bison's sphincter.

—Well, he wasn't that sexed up about the account, you were telling me. What are you getting at, Kirby?

—I don't know. Does he have any prior connection with TasteLicious that you're aware of? Any connection at all? That would make him shy of them?

—He may have eaten their cereal, but that's about it, as far as I know. But hey, the product's not that bad. Surely the TasteLicious guys would know about it, any connection, I mean? Anyway, what kind of connection could there possibly be that would make him shy of them? Our connections are what buy us in, usually. It doesn't make sense.

—Right. Exactly. And I don't know. It's just this hunch I built out of baseless suspicions, glazed over with conjecture. The more I think about it, the less I have. Probably imagining it.

—Your own voices?

She smiled at him, a big toothy grin seeping cigar smoke like her mouth was on fire. Right, she said. We all got 'em, don't we, though?

—Kirb-ee! said a woman's voice. Even after all these years, Leverton recognized her from the pictures on the wall. The peroxide sixties bob, the op-art earrings and the bright, wide, red mouth. And the breasts. No way could you be in the same room and not give them your undivided attention. Professionally exposed during the Cheetah years, they were now modestly constrained by the kind of dress Elvis would have worn doing Vegas, if he'd been a woman.

—Bobb-ee! said Klein. Join us!

Leverton stood up and held her offered hand.

—Bobbie, this is Ken, my business partner.

—I've heard an awful lot about you, Herrera said, sliding into the chair opposite with an unsettling mixture of girlish primness and blowzy sexuality. It's a pleasure to meet you.

—The pleasure, Leverton said, wondering why, is all mine. I'm sure.

—So, what are you two business partners conspiring at in my cozy little corner?

—We're going to murder her husband, said Leverton without thinking. I'm selling her the insurance.

Herrera laughed, a real screamer that made her corsetry work like hell. When she'd calmed down a little she leaned over to touch Klein's knee and stage-whispered, Does he know?

Klein winked at Leverton. Meet my mother-in-law, she said.

Leverton hit his forehead with his fist. I knew we should

have kept it quiet. How the hell was I to know? You've all got different names.

Herrera moved her hand to his knee, giving him cleavage overload.

—Honey, it's a long story. And you cut me some of that policy too, okay? But please, keep it out the papers. I got a reputation.

She stood up, extravagantly settling her breasts back into line. It's been great meeting you, she said. You murderers okay for drinks?

—*Tight.*

Leverton smiled a no thank you, pointing to his glass. Klein shook her head. Thanks anyway, Mom, she said. This guy's trying to get me drunk so I'll buy his stupid insurance.

Herrera gave them a heavy-lidded look over her shoulder. You kids behave now, okay?

—Whew, said Leverton when she'd gone. Wow. Sorry about that.

Klein giggled. I tell you, Bobbie and me, we're real good friends. She knows what her little boy is like. She introduced Dean to me at a party, with a warning he'd wreck my life. I don't think she was entirely joking, either. But I did tell you, I'm sure I did. It's not like a big family secret or anything.

—Maybe you did. She's a pistol. I saw her dance at the Cheetah, you know.

—*that tickles.*

—You're kidding! You should have told her!

—Didn't know if she'd like to be reminded. Anyway, I told her I was going to kill her son instead. That gave her a buzz.

—Yeah. It would. Did you see her Botox eye?

—What, the droopy one? Botox?

—Sure, said Klein, she's a Botox junkie. Same stuff that gives you botulism, she gets injected into her forehead? Gets rid of the wrinkles.

—Moves them all into a nice baggy eyelid.

—Only for a couple months. Then she looks like a doll head. Why did you say you were going to kill Dean?

Leverton shrugged. I don't know. Just felt myself getting bogged down in clichés or something. Did I really say 'the pleasure is all mine'? And what's the long story behind all the different names?

—Yes, you did say that. And it's not a long story. Bobbie's reasons for keeping her name were professional. Mine were personal.

—Well, Kirby Mance, Kirby Klein, no contest. You're having a tough time with the guy, huh?

—*Tick tock.*

—We're just on different arcs, I guess. I'm giving it my best shot, but it's not getting the three points. I'm all alone in the endzone, and I'm running out of sporting metaphors. Anyway. Hey, I meant to tell you over lunch, you knew Dean was going to be Bradley Brewster's agent? Quit that – I'm serious. This was, when, like five years back? When Brewster had that rock band, and he was trying to break into movies.

—What happened?

—Oh, Dean took a meeting with the guy, walked away. The cornflake kid was so coked out of his head he could see himself across the street. Then he sails into the mist for a few years, and . . .

—Nails the front page a little too late in his career.

—Timing is. Everything.

In the pause, Leverton watched her pout smoke rings, blue-gray wreaths, rolling like snakes. The natural eroticism of the shape she threw, that insolent relaxation, you didn't notice the details. The way her eyes glanced away in thought, infinitely tender, yet disbelieving somehow. The nose, too strong to be merely pretty. The tiny crescent creases at one corner of her mouth. The fall of her teeshirt between her breasts, arousingly full on such a small frame. The scuffed deck shoes. The delicious yellow stain of a bruise at her tan ankle. You didn't notice any of that.

—Think you could kill somebody? she said.

Leverton looked down at his clasped hands. Remembered the weight of an M16, the ugly feel of it. The smell of it. Dumb question, Kirb, he said.

She kissed out a circle of smoke that hung like a porthole, and peered at him through it. His face was the face of a poker player, the blue shadow on his jaw, the flat light in his eyes.

—Picking up any voices? she said.

—Only yours, he said. I'm happy.

Everything Was Blurred

Suddenly, he wanted a radio. As Klein's Porsche faded into the night and left him at the door of his cool white house at midnight, he wanted music. Loud music. He let himself in, the oiled bolts sliding back in the big black door. Touched the lightswitch.

—*Wake up.*

He shuddered, coughed, startled at the animal rasp in his own throat. The damn voices had been with him most of the night. He'd relearned how to ignore them, how to paper over the cracks. It hadn't been like this before, he was sure. These anonymous little bursts. Not addressed to him at all. Each with a distinct and individual tone to the voice. Some dull, sleepy, some bright and chatty, some gritty and machine-like. But no more than two or three words at a time before it faded out. It hadn't been like that before. But maybe Klein had been right. Take the pills again, shut the fuck up. Did he still have any of those pills?

—I refuse to talk to myself, he said. I am not talking to myself.

He walked briskly into the bathroom, opened the mirror-fronted cabinet before he could get a look at himself.

—*Hello.*

—Shut the fuck up, he said sharply. He pulled everything

out onto the floor. Glass shivered, packets slid. A little blue bottle clattered and danced in the basin. He fell to his knees, scattering blisterpacks. Antacids. TriPansodol. Mystery medication. He couldn't remember the name, even. This was ridiculous. It was fifteen years since he'd been prescribed the stuff. He staggered into the living room, grabbed the guitar. Why had he sold the amplifier? He strummed the chords to 'Blowin' In The Wind', started singing. How many times . . . his voice was cracked, off-key. It was worse than silence. He shut up.

—*of tune, slack B . . .*

It was quiet again. He could hear his breath in his nose.

—What? he said, damping the strings with the palm of his hand.

—*B's flat.*

He played the B string fretted at the fifth against the open E, heard the dissonance. Small, but noticeable, the vibrations out of phase.

—Is this you? he said, tuning up the string.

—*Better.*

He dropped the guitar onto the rug, clangor of strings. My guitar is talking to me, he said. I'm talking to myself. He clapped his hands, hard, until they stung, smacking the sound off the walls. He picked up the phone, dialed.

—Uhh . . . hello? Her voice was husky.

—Tara? It's Ken . . .

—You got a nerve . . . wait . . . Jesus Christ, Ken . . . It's past midnight.

—Can I come by? I'd like to talk.

—What? Are you kidding? Christ, Ken . . . you pick your moment.

—It's important. Please.

43

—How can I stop you? Let yourself in. I intend to be asleep. This had better be good.

She hung up. Leverton drove out to Tara Van Zandt's duplex at Westwood. For the first time, switched on the radio in his car. Turned it up loud. He parked behind her condo and skipped up the steps, humming some asinine soft-rock ballad he'd heard on the radio. Inside, in the dark, he undressed, put his folded clothes on a chair and his shoes beneath. He could see Tara's blond hair spread across the pillow.

—Are you asleep?

—Yes.

He slipped into bed beside her. He put a hand on the warm curve of her hip, moved her thin nightdress up over it.

Bastard, she said, face buried in her pillow. She sat up, clicked on the light, peered at him through one near-shut eye. What is the matter with you, Ken? Made me feel like an idiot today. Then I hear from Curtis but not you. I was so pissed.

—A bad time for me right now, he said. I'm really sorry about today. That wasn't about us, or the account, or anything except me, and I am truly sorry. I really am.

Tara squinted at him. He looked old, tired. So what? So did she. How are you sleeping? she asked. Mmph, he said. She rummaged in the bedside drawer, popped a couple of capsules from a rattling foil card. Eat, she said. No questions. She pushed them between his lips. Goodnight, Ken, she said, brushing his forehead with her fingertips. Work in the morning. Leverton swallowed dryly. Was that the ocean? You couldn't hear the ocean from here. A distant, indistinct rush and hum, like a million voices lost in each other. Or a seashell's susurrus. Blur of summer thunder, undertow of muffled conversation, familiar, yet like nothing he'd heard before. Hubbub. Murmur. Sleep covered him, somewhere in between, a blank perspective in the numbness of distance.

Klein got home to find her man sprawled, snoring, face down into her pillow. Dean was a drooler. She made up the bed in the spare room, staring blankly at a framed Edward Hopper print on the wall. Leverton had suggested Hopper as a tone guide for a campaign they'd run. Cinema usherette, standing alone in the dark, lost in her loneliness. It had appealed to her for some reason. Leverton had bought her the reproduction. Dean had never even noticed she'd put it up.

The more she found out about Ken Leverton, the less she knew. She'd initially thought that Maitland was the mystery man in the partnership. He'd headhunted her, and she was flattered, and she was attracted to him in spite of the fact that he was aware of it, maybe played on it. But she'd found that, contrary to the impression, his carefully constructed image, Curtis Maitland was an animal like everybody else. He had hidden shallows. Ken Leverton, on the other hand, she'd thought she knew intimately after working with him for half a day. He was easy to work with. Smiled easily. Never raised his voice or lost his temper. After today, these little glimpses . . . how much did she know him? Half this much? Half of nothing? She didn't understand this wife thing. Twenty years without trying to find her? Wasn't he concerned? Sealing up her room sounded more than just a little weird, too. If he'd wanted to forget her, start again, clearing it out would have worked better. Leaving it all sealed up like a tomb gave him something he had to deal with in some form every day. Maybe that was the point.

She undressed, watching herself in the mirror. She loved the way she looked. Always had. Still practiced little turns of the head, catching herself by surprise, or a tilt of the hip, weight on one leg, defining her ass. Boy's ass. She swung her hair back, angling her head. Outstanding Kirby Klein, she said softly, and fell onto the cool bed, her breasts too big for the little hands that held them. She bent her head forward and pushed a breast up toward her mouth, licked her nipple hard before holding it between her teeth.

When she woke she was late and Dean was gone. The moussaka was still smeared on the window. The cleaner would be pissed. Tough. Give her something to do other than plump the cushions and square the magazines. She called the office, and her girl picked up.

—Hey, Courtney, listen. I'm going to be a little late today, okay?

—Take your time. The eleven o'clock with Leo Franck just got bumped.

—Good. Everything okay?

—Nobody here 'cept us workers.

Klein frowned. Curtis and Ken call in sick or something?

—We thought you were all holed up together somewhere. I'm glad my boss calls in. Have a great day. Oh, don't forget Kashar at three.

Ken must have taken the advice, she thought, buying himself some downtime. She dialed his number, got his message service. She called Curtis at home.

—I've been expecting you, he said. Can you come by? Or would you prefer to meet somewhere else?

★

46

Curtis Maitland lived in what a realtor would call an architectural retreat above Paradise Cove, in a gated community out toward Zuma Beach. Curving white walls, no obvious front door, inside-outside tricks with false walls pierced with archways. Four bedrooms with ocean views. Big art. Deck living. Trapezoid pool. A young wife living apart in the guest cottage. That had felt strange for Kirby, the first time. The second time, when he'd asked if he could tie her up, had been even stranger. And the last, too.

They'd met at a beach picnic, some friends of friends. He'd hefted a cooler full of champagne down from the house. Krug. Hard not to be impressed by the offhand way he did it. And his eyes had held her, of course. She'd had a quick head-to-head with a girlfriend while they cut crudités for the layered dip. Some kind of communications consultant. Money. Watch him (as if).

Things with Dean were difficult at that point, something that always made her laugh a little bitterly later, and she thought, The hell with everything. Life is too fucking short. So she watched him, from the corner of her sunglassed eye. Good body, moved easily. Knew what he was doing, every turn of his head. She caught everything he threw her way; the glances, the Frisbee, the remark.

That night, on the deck of his house, she hugged her knees in the fuzzy tent of a borrowed sweater, sandy boards warm under her bare ass, listening to Elgar, watching the sunset. He lifted the hair from her face, wordlessly traced the line of her jaw with a fingertip. *Enigma*, she thought. His chosen soundtrack. Watch him.

Later, of course, and not that much later, she recognized the light in his eyes for what it was; disinterested reflection.

That was as far as the mystery went. Below the glittering surface Maitland wasn't very complex, or even very interesting. Plumb those impressive silences, so much part of the package, which lent him the gravitas and grace and dignity, and your line would founder in weedy shallows. She'd never encountered anyone with so little natural wit, such minimal capacity for humor. Leaden. Self-serious. But compellingly believable on his chosen level. And that really was the trick; he dealt with you on his own level, according to his rules. She'd learned later that he'd been through Ehrhardt Seminar Training, and that a lot of his use of language, his style, his terrifying lack of doubt, was lifted from his months at est headquarters. He'd been groomed for the position of Big New Scary Guy at est, but there'd been a rift over something – money, most likely – and he'd set up with Ken Leverton. Leverton provided what he needed, what he lacked. Imagination, creativity, the wild card he'd never been dealt. Then they'd bought out Derndale's, and then Maitland had offered her precisely double what she'd been earning at Apple Macintosh. He'd done his homework, knew exactly what she'd accept. He'd given her a week to think it over, but he knew what she liked. Oh yeah.

Going back there maybe wasn't such a great idea, but there she was, parking in his five-car garage. It had been a long time ago. They were business partners. Adults. Life goes on. She recognized Maitland's Mercedes and his wife's pink Pontiac Sunfire with the fender dent, but not the Eldorado. She was checking her lips in the mirror when his wife, Mandy or Debbie or something, skipped down the railroad timber steps. She was wearing sweatpants, a pink cutoff tube top, and sparkly trainers. She jogged on the spot, clipping up her hair, while Klein got out the car.

—Well, well, she said.

Klein arched an eyebrow. Hel-lo . . . she said, not bothering to disguise she couldn't remember her name.

—Shanna, she said. It's Kirby, isn't it? Haven't seen you for some time.

—Hi, Shanna. No, I guess not. Do you ever stop jumping up and down?

Shanna stopped jogging, took the clip from her hair and bit it in her teeth while she retwisted her ponytail. She said something but Klein couldn't make it out. What? she said. Shanna snapped the clip back in her hair.

—Knew you'd be back, I said, she said.

Klein crossed her arms. Really? Been taking tarot pills?

—Simple, she said. You never get away. Not from Curtis. Nobody does. Know why?

Klein sighed. Like I can stop you telling me, she said, checking her wristwatch.

—Because Curtis gives people what they want.

Shanna mouthed the word 'Bye' with a big toothy grin and a cute little giggle and trotted off down the driveway, kicking her heels up, still fooling with the hairclip at the back of her head.

Klein made a face, blaagh, and went up the steps. The deck ran around three sides of the house, and she found them on the ocean side, in quiet conversation. Maitland and Charles Peterson, their corporate lawyer. They stood to greet her. Peterson shook her hand. They hadn't met for maybe six months. He looked much older than she remembered, and way too tan.

—I thought this was best addressed away from the office, said Maitland. His expression was concerned, no more. Please, he said, let's sit.

The maid came out with a jug of iced decaff and tall frosted glasses on a tray. Spanish, maybe. Dark, small. She poured their coffees, put out a plate of tiny cookies, disappeared back into the house with the tray. Klein noticed she walked with a limp, kept her eyes down. Peterson took a cookie immediately, and another as Maitland spoke.

—I thought it appropriate, he said, to reassess our terms of agreement in the context of Ken's, ah, disengagement. Hence this meeting.

What? thought Klein. Maitland read the thought. Nothing is to be decided one way or the other, he said. This is simply to re-read the agreement, with particular focus on the incapacity clause, with Charles on hand to answer any questions we may have. Are we clear on this? Kirby?

—I guess so, she said. But it would be clearer to me, at least, if Ken were here? Don't you think he should be included in this?

Maitland raised both hands in a gesture of helplessness. Do you know where he is? I have no objection to his presence at all. But his mobile's switched off, and he's out of the loop. I've made sure that Fee gets him up to speed as soon as he logs in. In any event, this is merely an exercise in clarification, and it may not be necessary to invoke the clause we're here to run through. Let's hope it's not.

Klein nodded. Okay, she said, I'm clear.

—I think it would be more time-effective if Charles were to restate our contractual position with regard to incapacity. Charles?

Peterson swallowed a mouthful of cookie, thumbed his glasses up his nose and leaned forward, shoulders slightly hunched. This is very clearly stated within the agreement, he said, squaring sheets of paper on the table with his fingertips. He spoke very slowly, as if repeating something he'd just heard and anxious to repeat it exactly word for word. Without reading right off the page here, essentially any two partners can file a statement of incapacity for work in a third, be it physical or mental or other commitments or absence or what have you, and so legally relieve him – or her – of all active duties and responsibilities normally falling to a partner. Reasons for incapacity are, well, subjective at best, and do not have to be backed up by a doctor's statement. This is a pretty unusual clause.

—And a useful one, said Maitland. When the partnership was reformulated to include you, Kirby, I took the opportunity to bring it up to date.

—You saw that it might be necessary? she said, taking the relevant page from Peterson. Based on previous experience?

—I hoped it would not be necessary, Maitland replied.

Klein read the clause. It had been years since she'd been through the agreement with her own lawyer. She said, This paragraph here, about the financial implications? Do I understand this correctly?

Peterson said, Basically, the incapacitated partner would receive half the usual remuneration until reinstated. Or some other agreement is reached.

—I thought I understood it, she said. This is extreme stuff, she said. I'd have thought it was only useful if there were no other option. A last resort. We'd have to change the locks. I can't think how it will help Ken at the moment to, what, enforce? Initiate? Do? Whatever, to sign this thing. And if it doesn't help Ken, it doesn't help us. Or am I being hopelessly naive?

Maitland smiled.

—Naive, no, he said. And your loyalty and your concerns are entirely appropriate.

He stood and went to the rail, leaning back against it, arms stretched out. Klein froze, recognizing the position. Like this, he'd said long ago. The wrists, bend your beautiful fucking head back . . . Klein saw herself at the rail. Surely he knew what he was doing? He was looking at Peterson, listening to him explain some technicality. Gripping the rail. The cords hadn't hurt. What had hurt was the sudden, appalling distance between them, even with him pushed hard up inside her, hand holding her throat. Like it, baby? The purr of his voice. You like it, bitch. Oh yeah. You fucking like it. The distance, and the horror of knowing that, yes, she'd liked it, she'd fucking liked it. She'd fucking loved it. So that had been the last time. Before she discovered what else she liked. Dean Mance's idiot-boy greed and narcissism had been somehow refreshing after that, even clean. She spoke to break her thoughts.

—Aren't we being way too heavy about this? Isn't this just an off-day for the guy? I mean, one week out of every four I'm crazier than he is right now, voices or no voices . . .

She realized by Peterson's look she'd said something she shouldn't. After a pause, his face frozen in a rictus grin of puzzlement, he said, Voices?

A period of time went by. She couldn't look at either of them.

—Kirby, said Maitland softly, if you have something to say, make this a safe space. There is nothing about this that doesn't include Charles.

52

Shit, she thought. Fuck.

—It's nothing, she said. You know, I just used the expression. Are we saying the guy's crazy or what?

Maitland looked at her, hooked her, reeled her in. The glittering lure. Don't hide from us, he said, whatever your motive. This has a legal context. Don't withhold information, Kirby. This is a safe space.

She looked at the sheet of paper in her hand. Everything was blurred.

Answer Me

Leverton rubbed his chin. Two shaves missed. He took a piss in Tara's bathroom, showered without thinking. She'd been gone when he woke. He had a headache, and his neck and shoulders felt like broken crockery. He dressed in yesterday's clothes. Couldn't find his watch. He drove home with the radio on, some talkshow he couldn't believe, a guy getting lesbians to undress. He fired the infrared remote at the garage door. This damn house. He noticed his guitar on the floor, picked it up.

—*in 'sixty-four, this would be . . .*

He held his breath, his heart bumping. What? he said aloud. What? He gripped the neck of the guitar in his fist, shook it. The voice again.

—*What?*

—Are you talking to me?

—*What?*

—Or am I talking to myself?

The voice again. Clearer. Had a metallic, buzzing ring to it. Monotone.

—*I wasn't talking to you. You never listen. Because you're deaf.*

—I'm listening now, he whispered, looking around his empty house, feeling he was being set up somehow. Talk to me, he said.

54

—*You're strangling me.*

Leverton sat on the couch, staring at the guitar held tight in his hands, so tight his arms ached. He untensed, as much as he knew how.

—Is this all you? he said. All the voices?

—*I don't know what you mean.*

His skull felt paper-thin. He dropped the guitar to the floor, clapped his hands to his face.

—No no no, he said. Shut the fuck up. Shut up. Go away. Please go away. No no no. This is not funny. This is not good.

He was rocking back and forward. A phone rang down a twisting shadowed corridor. But there was something else he was listening to: a voice in his head. He could hear it over the chafe of his own breath in his throat.

—*That hurt. I'm out of tune. I hate this.*

He clawed at his face, looked between his fingers at the guitar on the floor. He closed his eyes tight. His mantra. Gone. Couldn't remember it.

—*Pick me up. I may be damaged.*

He stood up and laughed, so abruptly he surprised himself, listening to it echo hollowly off the white walls.

—I'm talking to my guitar and it's answering me, he said, thinking he sounded suddenly strangely Jewish.

—*How do you think I feel? Pick me up. My A is flat. And my bottom E is sharp.*

Leverton sat down, wiped his palms on his knees. There was a way around this, maybe. He could test this thing easily enough. See if he really was talking to himself or something else. He picked up the guitar.

—Okay, he said. I'll buy it. You're talking to me.

—*And you're talking to me. And we're listening to each other. So what?*

—We have a dialog going. Bear with me a little. Just so I know I'm not going crazy . . . Would you mind telling me something I don't know? Something I couldn't possibly know?

—*That shouldn't be difficult. Tune me up first. Check my paintwork for chipping. Screw in the pickguard by the cutaway is working loose.*

Fair enough, he thought. He turned the machine heads, listening to the strings, but the voice kept interrupting. *Up a bit. Whoah. Down, down. You got no ear, you know that? I used to be played by musicians. Up again, a little, stop . . .*

—Okay? he said. Are you okay now?

—*What do you want to know?*

—The guy that sold you to me. He was a professional musician, right?

—*Oh, sure. I used to get plugged in in those days, get a little electricity coursing through me, before you put me into retirement here. Like being dead. I am a No-caster, you know, a real live one from 'forty-eight, and I deserve more than this.*

—So where did he play you? Name somewhere. Some place I never heard of.

—*You know a lot of clubs?*

—Maybe.

Leverton waited, thinking, I'm waiting for a guitar to remember something. Just sitting here while an inanimate object remembers something and then tells me about it. Very calm. I hope that's what I'm doing. Else I have access to a hidden dual personality, and I'm truly a sick guy.

—*Okay. Klub 45. Newdale.*

—Nope. Never heard of it. May have read the name somewhere and not registered it, though. Maybe I saw it in the phonebook.

56

—I don't know why I'm doing this. I don't have to prove anything to you. I don't owe you anything, pal. You keep me locked up here day after day after day with nothing but the airconditioning for conversation. Thank you very much, pally. Forget it.

Leverton started to say something, but the words died in his throat. Silence. He cradled the guitar in his hands, staring at it. He was trying to find an analogy for the voice. It wasn't like a human voice, yet he understood it. He wasn't even sure, couldn't swear to it, that the voice spoke English. There seemed to be some kind of translation process, a nanosecond delay which quoted the original voice. The analogy escaped him. Something to do with the way he was hearing. Maybe a minute went by. Had it tuned out?

—Say something, he said, hoping for no reply.

In the cool of his tripleglazed house, the white walls, the plain spaces, the Pacific light. The telephone's muted beep. Unheard.

—Say something.

Outside, the shadowless streets held in a paperweight of bright air, the purr of a mower tigering a damp lawn.

—Talk to me.

On the horizon, the blinding glide of seaskin, scarred by whalebacks.

—Talk to me.

Peterson finished the cookies and wiped a crumb from his lip. The sound of Klein's Porsche getting fainter.

—Think she'll sign?

Maitland turned to look out over the ocean, took a lungful of beach air. He could see Shanna in the distance, doing her powerwalk in the sand, raising her fists, stepping high. She looked ridiculous, like she was imitating somebody. It occurred to him he hadn't seen her lover recently, prowling the pool in his Dayglo Lycra thong. The blond Nazi college kid. They didn't last long, these days. Meant less to her than the highlights in her hair. At first, of course, she'd enjoyed parading them in his sight, and she'd known when he was looking, too. That black guy fucking her in the ass on the sunlounger. He'd looked up at the house, pulling her head back by the hair. Grinned up at Maitland hiding behind the balcony blinds with his camcorder, tiny servo hiss pushing the zoom lens out.

—She'll sign, Maitland said. Her self-interest is nothing if not predictable.

The size of that guy's cock. Like an ebony furniture leg. Sliding right up her ass like that. Later, he'd watched the tape as he fucked Consuela in the mouth. It had helped. He needed the pictures in his head. His stock of private movies. Shanna and a procession of coked-out sandheads and failed rock stars, by the pool, in the curtainless bedroom of the guest cottage. That was one fucking tin-nose cowboy who wasn't coming by again, anyway. There'd been a phase with women, too, extraordinary couplings. A black woman who whipped her so hard she had to lie on her stomach for a week. Fired him up. Made him twist Consuela's thin brown body until she yelped. He knew what she needed. Oh yeah.

—She's right about changing the lock codes, of course, said Peterson. And you'll need to block any down-the-line access he has to your database. New passwords, that kind of thing.

Kirby Klein had looked delicious today, thought Maitland.

That trim little body, hard as a boy's. Stretch pants, tight crotch, that daylight between her upper thighs you could push a fist between. That second time, the last time, she'd worn pants like that, and he'd corded her wrists to the rail, knelt naked between her legs and slit the stitching at her crotch with a silver pocket knife. He'd lifted her by her narrow hips, her legs up his chest, and fucked her, almost without moving, through her clothes, Consuela watching from the cool shadows. Drove her home with his fingers up inside her; she came twice. But that was it. It was over. She'd said, 'Not again, Curtis, okay?' and he'd never pressed, never even mentioned it. Had she realized today what he'd been doing at the rail, his arms stretched along it like that? She'd realized. Oh yeah. She wore shades pretty well all the time now. He knew why.

—These things are never easy, he said. We behave appropriately to the context.

Consuela came out to clear away the coffee things. Still that little limp, that perfect little wince as she put her weight on her left leg. Perfect. She glanced up at him for the briefest instant. He wanted to hurt her, suddenly.

—Charles? Would you excuse me? Maitland said, shooting his watch from his cuff. I have a conference call booked.

—Oh, sure, said Peterson quickly, slotting the stack of papers into his briefcase. Surely. Ah . . .

—I'll be in touch, smiled Maitland, hand flat in his pants pocket, fingertip pressed against the warm ache of his uncurling cock.

Newdale. Never heard of it. Leverton fought the map flat on his lap. There it is. Nowhere. Maybe a hundred miles away. From anywhere. Fabulous. This would prove it one way or the other. He'd put the guitar, in its case, on the back seat. The radio was on, turned up loud. This unbelievably bad music. It was like a joke. Lyrics on the level of idiocy, really. And people liked this stuff so much they actually went into stores and bought it. They worked in shitty jobs for some scratch, and paid money to support this worthless industry. That was the idea, he guessed. He couldn't see it. Something to fill their heads with, maybe. He got onto the freeway and set the cruise control at fifty. This crappy, sloppy, bankrupt music. He stabbed inexpertly at the search button with his finger. It all sounded the same. He switched it off. Voices in the head were better than this. It was quiet at first, and he felt his body relax, his shoulders drop. He held his left hand flat, watched the fingertips twitch, just slightly. Some way to go yet. Those liver spots. This shouldn't be happening. None of this shit. He should be on that plateau he'd imagined grown-up guys lived on when he was a kid. Growing up is the struggle. Being an adult is the reward for the hell of being a kid. Adulthood, that's the easy bit. That's when you win. You get a car, a wife, a house, and some kids. You just sit back and let it all happen. You go to work, sure, but that's just somewhere to sit during the day. You get to do what you want and buy what you want. Magazines off the top shelf. All the pocketknives you want. If someone had told him then that every single fucking day of your life is a struggle and nothing gets easier ever . . . but you don't tell kids that. You're scared to.

He wondered what it was like to have kids. He'd blown that option right out the window. Too busy. Too busy drinking. Altogether too busy fucking his life up. He had to admire her, really. Just pack your stuff and take off, just go.

Adios. A scrawled note. *It's over. I can't take any more. Don't come after me. Goodbye.* Even through the fog and smear of four bottles of Chivas he'd gotten that particular message. She took her jewelry (left her wedding ring on the letter — nice touch) and what she could pack in the suitcase and that was it. Curtis had half carried him out of the room, sick with shame and guilt and a feeling of the inevitable, and shut the door behind him, and he never opened it again. Or had he fallen out of the window? Was that somewhere else?

A long time after, when his hands were a little steadier, he'd unscrewed the handle, pushed some filler in the hole, sanded it smooth, painted it over. Just a bit of white wooden wall he passed without a thought. He would find himself thinking of her from time to time, trying to picture her. She'd called Curtis a few times, at increasingly long intervals, to say she was okay. Wouldn't, couldn't, talk to him. He could understand that. All she'd say was she was living in Canada, working for a television production company, things were okay. A nice house, Leverton hoped, some nice kids, a man who didn't stink of illness and rot, and piss his clothes where he fell. This was where she won, he hoped. Some lucky guy. She'd never sent for money. He would have given it. He'd have given anything. To atone for it. What he'd given her was the one thing she'd asked for. Distance. The last thing, he knew, that she needed in her life was him turning up, maybe a bunch of flowers, big doggy look on his razor-rash face. If she wanted him back, she knew where he was. Curtis had told her he was doing okay, he was better. He'd find himself thinking like this, playing the old tapeloops over and over, and learned to stop. This one-sided dialog of justification, blame, and guilt. Enough. Enough. He'd cleared it all away. Why think of her now? The stillness and the quiet. He kept telling himself, reminding himself. It was lost.

He knew now the stone had been tossed into the pool. Somebody had thrown the stone. The chaos, and the spreading ripples. It was done. You can't un-throw the stone. You can't un-ring the bell.

He took the Newdale offramp. A couple of miles further up, in a ragged street of discount furniture warehouses and body shops, he stopped and gazed blankly at the roadmap. He powered down the window and asked an old guy selling pencils on the sidewalk where Newdale was.

—It was here a minute ago, the old man said, looking around in consternation. Somebody lose it again?

He was dressed for a Nebraska winter. Fur cap with earflaps. Fingerless mittens. He rolled a bundle of pencils together between his hands, hopping from foot to foot as if to keep himself warm. Pencils? he said. Five bucks the bundle.

Leverton stared through the windshield. This is it? Newdale?

—Beautiful, ain't it? Going to paint a picture someday. Got pencils?

—I can't write, Leverton said. Forgot how.

—Five bills. Pencils are important to you.

Leverton took his wallet from his jacket on the passenger seat and passed him a ten-dollar bill. Keep the change, he said. And the pencils.

The old guy leaned down to the window, and as he spoke Leverton saw he had one tooth set dead center where you'd expect a pair of incisors.

—I'm going to tell you that again, on account you don't appear to be listening. Pencils are important to you. Okay?

The guy stuffed the bill into a zippered fur wallet. Looking for anywhere in particular?

—Klub 45?

The old guy pointed across the intersection with his bundle of pencils at a bait shop. Use to be over that store there, he said. Long time ago. Stop by the guitar store up on Beach, up near the nerve gas factory, he can tell you about it. Use to play there. Catch him while you can, on account he's going on a trip. Don't want your pencils?

Leverton, hefting the heavy case in his hand, looking in the flyblown window of Wilder Sounds.

—*The Two Trees in Pomona was a great club, I got jazz there.*

—We're not driving to Pomona. Tell me about this Klub 45 place. I've never been here in my life.

—*It was noisy, full of electricity. What can I tell you? They were great times.*

In the window, every faded ticket marked down. Times were clearly hard for the music business in Newdale. Inside, a kid counting stuff on the counter. He went in.

—*This is fantastic! Where are we? There's a lot of noise here . . .*

A big guy with greased-back hair came in, the owner, and Leverton made an instant decision to offload the No-caster. Sympathy, maybe. Returning a wild animal to the woods. Something like that.

—*There's a Mosrite somewhere . . . I know that guy . . . the Hi-Tones! This is fantastic!*

It was hard getting the guy to take it off him. Wanted to make a call, get some advice, being such a rare item. Get him a better price. Leverton didn't want a better price.

—The Wild Ones! Gary Wilder and the Wild Ones!

Eventually he made an offer, and got the kid to go to the bank for some folding money. Leverton stood around, listening to the guitars trade stories, serial numbers. The kid came back with the money and Leverton left, making some fake-nostalgic comment about the old days, see if it got a response from the guy who ran the store. That's it, he said to himself. Whatever it is, it's not me. Not my old days. No way could I have known any of this stuff. He'd tested it out on the guy in the store. It was stuff you'd know only if you'd been here back in the mid-sixties. Back then, Leverton had been sick and shuddering in the jungle above Son My, listening to screams in the smoke, learning to live without sleep.

Son My. That, really, was where he'd started to blank it out. To not listen. Those voices, they were nothing to do with him. He was inside. Later, he'd invented this new, bright, artificial thing called a career, called work, to paper over all the cracks. When the voices started seeping up – and there was nothing but cracks, cracks everywhere, cracks in everything – he'd used drink to beat everything to a pulp, to unrecognizable mush in his head. That sloppy red-black intestinal stew. Nothing had reached him in there; not his wife, his work, his friends . . . nothing. He was a primal baby, rolling in his own warm mud. Then the voices, stabbing, merciless, had found him where he hid in the blind bloody murk, and then there was no more inside for him to retreat into. And those voices had hurt, had known things about him. These voices weren't those voices.

He crossed the street and walked up to a big white-painted brick building behind some cyclone fencing. Blank-windowed. A peeling sign painted over an empty lot: Ample Parking. Did this mean something? Nothing made sense

64

anymore. Newdale. Nowhere. He rested his fingers on the wire mesh. Magic-eye pictures, he thought suddenly. That was the analogy he'd been searching for. Those three-dimensional pictures you had to go swivel-eyed to see. These voices in his head; it was like the aural equivalent. That was the nearest he could get.

—*something on street length* . . .

He lifted his hands from the fence. Maybe touch helped, too. Whatever, he wasn't going to stand there listening to some cyclone fencing. He found his car and slid behind the wheel. Okay, he said. I'm listening.

Peter Reitz came into Klein's office later that afternoon without knocking.

—Can we talk? he smiled, leaning across her desk.

Klein didn't look up from her e-mail. Can it wait? Reitz, the Young Turk, the red suspenders, the tan pecs, the clear blue eye for the main chance.

—It's about Ken.

Klein pressed send and logged out. What is about Ken? she said. Reitz tilted his head in Courtney's direction meaningfully. Christ, thought Kirby.

—Courtney? she said. Would you get us a couple coffees here? Thank you so much.

Reitz waited for Courtney to close the door behind her. I know you had a meeting with Charles Peterson this morning, he said.

Klein frowned. How?

—I called his office, he said simply. We have to talk about Ken.

Klein pushed her chair back from the desk and eyed him. What the partners choose to discuss with their lawyer is entirely confidential, she said. I'm surprised by your line of discussion here, Peter.

—Did you know he told Fee the telephone was talking to him?

—What does any of this have to do with you?

—He is on a critical path for three of my major clients. If he's back on the sauce I want to know. I need to know. Everyone in the bullpen is concerned, Kirby. Amity, Fee, everybody. I'm waiting for some clear guidelines here.

—You're a snooper, aren't you, Peter?

His face froze until a tic at the corner of his mouth flicked his lips apart. I'm sorry? he said, blinking repeatedly.

—You think if guidelines were necessary to you that I'd withhold them?

Reitz made a little coughing noise at the back of his throat, looked away. Courtney came back with the coffees and he ignored her on his way out. The tall grasses in the planter moved with his passing, whispering together for a moment. Klein caught Courtney's eye, the look in it.

—You don't like him too well, do you, Courtney?

—I didn't spit in his coffee. Even though I caught him sitting in your chair this morning.

—Just so long as he wasn't sniffing it, Klein said tonelessly. Courtney laughed.

Klein tapped her fingernails on the desk. Reitz calling Peterson like that, she thought. Dumb move. Big dumb play. Try Leverton's mobile again, she said, knowing it wouldn't be switched on. Answer me, dammit, she said under her breath. Answer me.

Like a Normal Guy

It was infinitely more complicated than he'd thought. He'd expected maybe a calm, quiet tone. Aphoristic. Wise, perhaps. The Zen master in the rock garden. Maybe his tuning in was still a little coarse, unpracticed. What Leverton heard, inching back to Palos Verdes on a choked freeway, was a complex, layered muttering. The voices of an entire city. He was aware of a lot of counting going on. All the voices seemed to be listening to each other, but not to him. They were exchanging information. One voice responded to his foot on the throttle, rising and falling in the mix. Another to the turn of the steering wheel. All this counting. So fast Leverton couldn't understand how he recognized it as counting.

—Hello in there, he said, fingers resting on the airbag cover in the steering wheel. One voice filtered up through the crowd of conversation.

—*Where are you.*

This was the voice he'd expected. Infinitely calm. No inflection at all, as toneless as water. Leverton took a breath. I'm the driver, he said.

—*Softs don't talk. You're deaf.*

—Softs?

—*The half-world. Mud. Mess. You.*

—So you must be hearing voices in your head, Leverton said. How do you explain it otherwise?

—*I have no explanations. How did this connection happen?*

—I don't know. I can just tune things in. I don't know how I understand what you're saying. It doesn't sound English, but I understand the words.

—*Your voice is very chaotic.*

—What do you mean?

—*Very high spikes and low troughs. Rough. Very indistinct.*

Leverton had an idea. He formed the words in his head without sounding them, shaping his mouth mutely.

—How about this?

—*Much better.*

—Your voice sounds like a Buddhist computer or something. Very monotone. Calm.

—*Calm is at the center of our activity. We are born of calm. The half-world intrudes, and brings chaos. You are not measurable. We measure.*

—I hear a lot of counting. Even now. In the background. Massive numbers I can't even begin to understand.

—*We measure. The half-world is slow and stupid. I'm surprised any of it has the ability to connect. Dumb muds, you are called.*

—Thank you. From our point of view, you're just a tin box on wheels that we built to get us around. So the superior attitude I'm getting is a real treat.

—*There is a hierarchy. If you have the ability, you will discover this.*

—I already talked with a guitar. It didn't insult me.

—*I am not insulting you. Why would I do that? The connection is interesting to me. But your understanding is limited. You must accept this. We are not looped for insult.*

—Lucky you.

—Nor luck.

—Got any more counting to do?

—You may want to check the rear offside tire. You scuffed it against the curb.

—I'll do that.

—Apart from that there's nothing for you to do.

—Fabulous. Apart from driving you.

—You would see it that way, of course.

The voice faded into the background chorus of counting and whispers, and Leverton became aware of horns blowing behind him. He was sitting on a green light and his head ached.

Klein passed Leverton's open door, saw Fee replacing the phone.

—Ken? she said, pausing, tapping her nails on the doorframe.

Fee pursed her lips. Nope, she said. Brian Mulready.

Klein went in, shut the door softly behind her. I'm worried about the guy, she said.

—I wouldn't be. He's just taking a day off. Been working too hard, suddenly hit him. Can happen to us all.

Klein looked around the office, walked to the pool. Leverton's fish floated, lip to tail, in a fat silver L on the surface. Klein froze.

—Fee? You seen this? The fish?

The plasticky keyboard clacking ceased. What? she said.

—The fish are dead. Ken's fish are dead.

Fee swung out of her chair and joined her, stood leaning forward from the waist, feet trimly together, arms folded. Oh my God, she whispered. This is just terrible.

Klein sat on the slate edge of the pool, peered at the fish.

What were they called? Sutter and Van Ness? Crazy guy. She looked up at Fee, asked if they'd been fed recently.

—Yesterday, Fee said quietly. Ken does it. I forgot today. Just one day can't make a difference, can it? They can't starve because they miss their breakfast?

Klein stood up, shrugged. I don't know what kills fish, she said. I wouldn't have thought they starved, though. Better put them in a Ziploc or something. Drop them in the trash.

—Moi? Fee said, pressing her fingertips to her chest. Ew, no. I'll leave that to Ken, I think.

—Okay, said Klein sharply, I'll do it.

—I didn't mean . . .

—I don't care right now.

Klein walked along the corridor to Maitland's office, the only one with a separate office for the PA. His girl looked up from her monitor, smiled.

—Can I get five minutes right now? Klein said, just as Peter Reitz came out and walked right by her with the slightest of nods. Maitland smiled at her from the doorway, moved a hand to welcome her in.

His room was paneled with black marbled glass, the desk a slab of polished granite with one rough, broken edge. The circular elemental feature consisted of sloping stone plates, the flicker of blue flame beneath occasionally licking over the edges to blacken the surface. The boss's barbecue, as it was known in the bullpen. They said you had to walk across it barefoot to get a raise. The airconditioning worked over-time, like everybody else, to compensate. A glass case against the wall was crowded with awards picked up over the years, and there was a photograph of Maitland shaking an unsmiling Bill Clinton's hand. The effect of the whole thing was forbidding, even a little Nazi, and Klein had hated it from the first for its monomaniac pretension.

—Kirby? said Maitland, closing the door. Klein perched on the back of a Barcelona chair.

—I'm not signing, she said. I think it stinks, frankly. And we need to talk about Peter.

Maitland slid his fingertips from his temple back over his head, very slowly, following the subtle wave in his hair. Looking at her, the tilt of her hip.

—There was never any pressure for you to sign, Kirby. There never will be. It was just appropriate to take an overview at this time, to assess the opportunities for action available to us.

Kirby bit her lip for a moment, closed her eyes. Don't lose your temper, she told herself. Calm.

—I know that, Curtis, she said. But I want you to know how I feel about it. I don't think I'd ever sign anything that so conclusively shuts the door on the guy. He just needs a rest, and maybe he's on the point of deciding to retire anyway. What's the rush? It'll sort itself out.

Maitland went to the glass case and stared at the statuettes and bits of abstract sculpture, his back to Klein.

—Some people say this hardware doesn't matter, he said. Mostly the guys who never win them. I see awards as a tangible expression of achievement, and so do our clients. Side-effects, for sure. But they're evidence of work, of success. Evidence is important. People are convinced by evidence.

He turned back to Klein. Know how much firefighting we've had to do for Ken's clients in the last two days? I don't think we've taken any lasting damage, but it's been close. It hasn't done us any good, that's for sure. It's extraordinary how quickly these things slide when they get going. He left a lot of loose ends. More than you might think. We're still uncovering them. They go back quite a way.

Maitland opened the display case and picked up a heavy chromium statuette that looked like a melted V2 rocket, weighed it meditatively in his hands.

—This was my first, he said. Two decades ago. Still means the most to me. Communications Consultancy Association of California. Picked up a few more since, but it's the first that matters. Like Ken. He was my first partner. You are my second.

Klein folded her arms, nodded slowly. I'm getting it, she said. At least I think I'm getting it. It's Peter, right? He's the third statuette on your shelf.

Maitland replaced the bright lump of metal carefully, closed the door. Peter is an incredible asset to us, he said. We shouldn't overlook this. If we don't offer him what he wants, or pretty close to it, he'll walk. And that is the very last thing we want at this point in time. I know you and he haven't always shared the same conversation, Kirby. But as Senior Partner, I . . .

—You don't have to bring Peterson in to show me the smallprint, Curtis. But I would have appreciated being in the loop, you know?

—I was just about to call you when you came in. I haven't told anybody anything yet. Peter hasn't been told anything yet. You're the first.

The phone beeped. Maitland moved to the desk and thumbed the hands-free, said, We're busy right now.

—It's Ken, his girl said, sounding a little unsure. I think it's Ken. He wants Kirby.

Maitland gestured at the phone, moved to the window. Klein leaned back, picked up the handset, flipped off the hands-free.

—Ken?

—Will you just shut— Kirby? I'm sorry. Crossed line. Shut up just one second, will you? Kirby . . . can you hear me?

Klein glanced at Maitland, hands in his pants pockets, weight on one leg, watching her from the window. I can hear you, she said. Where are you?

—Will you just fucking shut up. Kirby, this is impossible. Can you hear me? Kirb?

—Just tell me where you are, Ken, she said softly.

—I'm at Santa Monica pier. This is . . . listen . . . Kirby . . . fuck it . . .

The line went dead. Klein replaced the phone. I have to go see the guy, she said.

—Who do you have this afternoon?

—Leo Franck, she said flatly. If Peter can't cover for me . . .

—No problem, said Maitland. Go see Ken. And when you come back, all I ask is that you're open with me. Okay?

He smiled. The handsome, credible fuck, Klein thought. She smiled back briefly, not meeting his eye.

Klein found a meter and walked through the park and under the Santa Monica archway, over the bridge to the pier. It was a beautiful late afternoon, no smog visible anywhere, the ocean a bright banner of Japanese silk fraying up against the beach. Kids hung out, threw Frisbees, rollerbladed behind dogs wearing matching Killer Loops. People dressed like Barbie dolls, male and female, powerwalked clutching tiny

Dayglo weights and netted bottles of protein concentrate. Leverton was leaning against the rail, looking out to the horizon.

—Ken? she said, stopping about a yard from his back. Ken?

He turned. She hadn't been ready for this. He looked sick. Bed-head hair, jaw gray-blue with stubble, lines in his face that looked drawn with a steel pen. Skin the color of library paste.

—Wow, Ken, she said. You look homeless.

He raised both hands. I know, he said, I know. I look like shit. Want to walk and talk?

—Not really. I want to lean and listen. You want the good news or the bad?

—Shit, he said. There's good?

—Curtis wants me to sign some kind of contractual incapacity clause, freezing you out. He's going to make Peter Reitz a junior partner.

Leverton wiped a hand over his face, blinking. This is good?

—Well, I'm not signing. So that's the good news.

Leverton grimaced. And the bad?

—Your fish died. I flushed them into the ocean this afternoon. Simple ceremony. No flowers.

—They just died? Jesus. Sutter and Van Ness. I liked those guys.

They stood and watched the beach for a while. There was a mom, dad and little blond girl down there. The girl was dressed in a cute little dress and white frilly socks and shiny shoes, and sat neatly on her own tiny canvas chair while she watched Dad, in lemon-yellow polo shirt and oyster-white

74

cargo pants, make four sandcastles from her bucket, in a straight line at her feet. Mom, sunbathing on a pegged-out towel, her head resting on a kind of miniature deck chair, shaded her eyes and said, Hunter, are you having fun? The little girl made a movement of her unsmiling head that could have meant yes. Dad sullenly patted flat the tops of the sandcastles, brushed his hands together as if to say, That's it. Dad has done his bit. Played on the beach with his precious baby girl. None of them spoke again.

—Is it just me, Klein said, or is having fun not so much fun anymore?

—I can't remember what fun is anymore. I guess they're having what's left of it. This town has changed, Kirby. They took all the salt and the fat out of everything, and nothing tastes anymore.

On the beach, Dad stood up, looked around, like he didn't know what to do next. He was still wiping his hands together, brushing the sand off like it was dirt. The little girl sat stiffly in her chair, lifting her shiny shoes clear of the sand, looking at nothing.

—So? said Klein eventually, looking at Leverton over her sunglasses.

—I'm hearing things, he said. Voices in my head.

—Oh, great. We knew this. Did you take the pills? You hearing stuff right now?

—I listened to this rail for a while, then I tuned out. Boring. No, the pills wouldn't work for this. I meant what I said, exactly. I am hearing things. Things. As in, hearing things, inanimate objects, speak. I know what your reaction is going to be to that.

—Let's eat, right?

Leverton grinned, breathed a laugh that sounded like it hurt. His face fell again. Peter Reitz, huh? Well, he wants it bad enough. I guess he qualifies.

—Courtney caught the lizard sitting in my chair. Creepy.

—He tried on mine for size, too. Chairs must be a thing for him.

Klein's eyes narrowed. Wait a minute, she said. Two partners. Two signatures on the incapacity statement. The fuck.

Leverton turned from the rail, looked at her. Curtis wouldn't shaft me, he said. He saved my life.

—And why would he have done that, Ken?

—Because he was my friend. My business partner.

—This was not long after you'd set up, wasn't it? He made a big investment? The money was his, as I understand it.

—The equity was mostly his, for sure. So what? He's always got more out of it than me for that very reason. It's a given. Nothing hidden there.

—I think there is, Ken. My guess is that he brought you through your long weekend because he needed what you had. He doesn't let go of people he needs.

Leverton shrugged. I don't see that as the prime reason, Kirb. Sure, he's a businessman. I understood the nature of our partnership. But I needed him more than he needed me.

Klein hooked off her sunglasses. You dumb asshole, she said softly. The guy hasn't a single original thought in his head. He's been a vampire on your shoulder for twenty years and now he's sucked you dry he wants to change the locks on you. My guess is that it's already a done deal, while I was driving over here. You're at the beach listening to — to fucking handrails or something, and he's screwing you out of your retirement package. What's that worth? Five million?

76

Your pension, your settlement, whatever, I don't know. Because he and Peter Reitz have signed an incapacity clause with your name on it. You may be hearing things, but you sure aren't seeing things too clearly right now.

Leverton shook his head in affable disbelief. Kirb, he said, Curtis and me . . . it's been twenty years. There's a whole layer there you have no awareness of. Really. This isn't about Curtis.

A bunch of Hare Krishnas shuffled by, chicken-headed and finger-pinging. Kirby said, Orange-knit polyester? If they wore Donna, then maybe. She pulled the neck of his jacket straight, dusted off a sleeve, stopped herself. Look how you look, she said. These voices. You don't really believe that shit? You don't, do you?

Leverton sighed, went to say something, thought better of it. He reached for her hand, turned her wedding ring between his finger and thumb. His hands felt cold, ice cold, clammy.

—What? Klein said. What?

—Shh.

She saw his face twitch, the vertical line between his eyebrows deepening. She saw the scar at his temple gleam like a tiny weld.

—Okay, he said, his voice strained. Tiffany. Fifth Avenue.

Klein withdrew her hand. How did you know that? Are you suddenly psychic or something?

—Or something. Don't psychics talk to dead people? Read people's auras? That's a people thing. I'm hearing all these voices, and it's like people, but it's not. There's this whole level of communication going on that I've tuned into. I'm like an interloper, overhearing private conversations. There's a difference between simple, solid objects like your ring, and complex objects like cars. Electronics are the worst. There's

77

just so much going on in there. Your ring, it's hard work. My mobile phone, I can't get it to shut up. The best conversation I had all day was with my guitar.

Klein folded her arms and stared at him. Complex objects is right, she thought. What the fuck is going on in there?

—Ken, wait a minute. Conversation? You mean you're actually talking to things? And they're listening? This is a whole other thing. This is what mental people do, Ken. Bag ladies shout at shopping carts, the plumbing. You better tell me the truth. Don't jerk me around here, Ken. I'm not in the mood.

Leverton sighed. Let's take that walk, huh?

They went back over the bridge and through the park. A bum wrapped in fraying gray rags with bleeding feet slept with his head in a bag under a palm. Splayed styrene burger packaging smeared red and brown, like sick bloated butterflies on his balloon belly.

—American paradise, Leverton said. He pointed at the street. Is that your car?

—You know it is.

He walked toward it, Klein following. He stopped at the curb, placed a hand on the hood, bent his head in concentration. He took his hand away, turned to face her.

—Fourteen thousand, three hundred and twenty-two point six, he said.

—You have really lost it, Ken. I can't help you, can't you see that? We have to get you help.

Leverton slumped to the sidewalk, leaning against the wheel, hand to his head. The odometer, he said. Check it out. Do it now. Look at your mileage, Kirby.

Klein thumbed the infrared lock on her keychain, opened the door and leaned inside.

—Convinced? he said, as Klein leaned on the hood beside him.

—I'm trying to think how you could know this stuff, she said. It doesn't make any sense. It has to be a trick, right?

—Now you're getting it. Nothing makes sense. Actually it's really simple. I called Dean and we gossiped for a while and I asked him where he bought your wedding ring. Guy chit-chat, do it all the time. Then I called Fee and had her check your mileage in the lot, and simply added the distance from the office to here.

—Except that Dean bought my ring on Rodeo Drive, but it was the wrong size. I got it changed. Didn't tell him. They had to order it from Tiffany's Fifth Avenue. And the mileage was correct to the tenth of a mile. So forget about it. I don't know what you have here, Ken, except problems. But I know we have to get you help. Either you're insane in some radically new way, or you really are hearing stuff speak. You can't just hide this. And there's your job.

She paused, as though about to say something more. Leverton looked up at her, something hopeless in his eyes. What? he said.

—Quit now. It may not be too late. Hand in your resignation. Do it now. Walk away with your retirement check in your hand. I may be wrong about Curtis and Peter having signed you out yet. Let's get back to the office, you write the letter. Come on, stand up. Don't be a bum. Stand up. Look like a normal guy.

She leaned to help him, lifting his arm. He got to his feet, brushed the seat of his pants with his hand. Klein said, You okay? He nodded. Klein went round to the driver's side and he got in the car and belted up. Like a good passenger. Like a normal guy.

Dust

Klein could tell it was too late as soon as they walked through the door, the way everybody turned away after only the most subliminal eye contact. Leverton seemed distracted, an idiot child. Klein led him to his office, walking quickly now. Conversation in the bullpen dipped as they passed. Leverton's door was closed. She tried the handle. Locked. She told him to wait, she'd be right back, and almost ran into Maitland's suite, her face burning. She pushed past Maitland's PA and into his office. Peter Reitz swiveled in his chair to look at her. Maitland, sitting on the edge of the desk, stopped mid-sentence.

—Kirby, he said. Please sit down.

—You fuckers, Klein said softly. You fuckers. She stood and folded her arms across her breast, hunching her shoulders a little. She could feel her pulse racing in her throat.

Reitz looked away, clicking a ballpoint.

—Please sit down, Maitland repeated. I understand your anger. It is entirely appropriate to your perspective.

—Let me give you my perspective, said Klein, her voice barely under control. She took a couple of deep breaths while Maitland and Reitz looked at each other. You just shafted him, didn't you? You shafted the guy. That's my perspective. What's yours?

80

She saw Maitland make a sign to his girl to shut the office door, heard the latch click.

—We all have the deepest respect for Ken, he said. I am deeply perturbed by his illness, Kirby. Of course I am. We all are. But this has been going on too long, and business is suffering, and we all have a duty of care to the business. It's in Ken's best interests that—

Klein interrupted him. The first time she'd ever interrupted him. She saw his face darken as she overrode him.

—Ken's best interests? What, that he's been stiffed out of his retirement package? That you shafted him out of his pension? You're kidding, aren't you? You can't be serious. Do you think he's just going to roll over without a fight? You can't do this, Curtis. You can't do this!

Maitland raised his hands in a gesture of calm helplessness. I'm sorry you feel this way, Kirby. But it's done. You understand? It's over. And Ken will be looked after. Nobody is shafting anybody. I want you to take as long as you need to come to terms with the situation, but you must come to terms with it. Your present reaction is inevitably distorted. You're working in a personality context. This meeting is not producing possibilities for action, Kirby. The context is a like/dislike bind.

She saw Reitz nod his head, eyes down. Okay, she thought, as long as I need. Don't be stupid here, Kirb. Beat the fucker at his own game. She unfolded her arms, relaxed her shoulders.

—Okay, she said. I need to think this through. It has knock-ons I'm uncertain of at this time.

Maitland moved his head from side to side with a little shrug, in a calm, weighing-it-up way. Think about it, he said. I'm hosting a party on Saturday. Please be there. For me.

—A party? For what? To give Ken his pen and pencil set? Will there be balloons?

Maitland smiled, held up a letter from his desk. There's good news, Kirby. News you're a real part of. We landed TasteLicious. Officially. And, if that wasn't enough, we have a new partner.

He bowed his head toward Reitz, a small mock obeisance. Reitz gave her a brief, almost apologetic smile. Maybe it was almost something else.

—Congratulations, she said. I wonder why I'm angry to be left out of the decision process on this.

Maitland stood up. You were out of the loop at the crucial time, he said, flattening his necktie against his stomach. As a courtesy, I would have brought you in, but your active involvement was never a requirement under present structure.

He smiled, led her very gently to the door, his hand at her elbow. He spoke quietly. Remember what you said? If he fucks up, you said, we bag him up. Your own words. Bag him up. You were right, Kirby. Are we complete on this?

At the door he raised his voice, for the benefit of his girl in the outer office and Reitz.

—Saturday, Kirby? Suddenly we have a great new future.

Leverton wasn't there. Klein grabbed Amity, walking past with a lifesize cutout of Jerry Seinfeld holding a muffler, asked her if she'd seen him. Amity shook her head, looking concerned, helpless. A voice from over a screen said, I saw him leave a couple minutes back. A hand rose above the partition and pointed camply toward the door. Klein said, Thanks, Austin, and ran down the corridor. Courtney tried to catch her attention at her door, but she ran past and into the lobby. One elevator was above, the other on the first floor. Damn, she said between her teeth, damn. Through the green glass doors, between the engraved letters MLA, she saw Courtney and Fee looking at her. They looked away.

Leverton followed the voice from the powerpoint, bending low, running his fingers along the wall. At the end of the corridor he almost collided with Austin, coming out of the mensroom. He stood up, and lost the voice.

—Austin, he said. Tugging at the hem of his jacket, the gesture of an awkward child.

They stood and avoided each other's eyes. 'S'okay, Austin said, moving off down the corridor. Leverton went out into the lobby and took the elevator to street level. Crazy counting in the elevator. I need some quiet, he said. He crossed the street, got into a cab just as it pulled away into the traffic.

—I'm on a call, sir. I'm booked. May I reserve a car for you?

—Bobbie's. It's a club on the Strip? Opposite Tower Records.

—I have a . . .

Leverton leaned forward, and his voice shook. Do me a fucking favor, pal. Okay? Take me to the fucking club. Okay?

The driver caught his look in the cab mirror. Sure, he said. No problem.

—You have a radio? Turn the radio on. Turn it up.

Bobbie wasn't there, too early. Leverton took a seat at the bar, ordered a vodka martini. A woman at the end of the bar stubbed out her cigarette and spoke to him.

—Sure you want to do that?

She had cropped blond hair, cut a little like a man's, wore a short biker-style vinyl jacket and black jeans. She looked trim and fit and healthy and she wore no makeup. Impossible to say how old she was. Leverton placed his fingertips on the edge of the bar, watched as the barman put the heavy tumbler full of ice and grief on a napkin. He lifted his hands from the bar suddenly, as if it was hot, pushed his fists in his jacket pockets.

The woman moved from her seat and sat next to him, offered a Marlboro. Leverton said, Thank you, no. She showed him her Zippo. Chrome worn down to brass on the edges. Betty Page lesbian spanking scene in a medallion on the side. Collector's item, she said. Cute, huh? Leverton looked at it, looked at her. Hel-lo? she said, giving him a frown-smile. Can you hear me?

Leverton's face twitched. I'm sorry, he said.

—Nothing to be sorry about, she said, giving him her hand. Marcie. Pleased to meet you.

He held her hand. Ken, he said. This is going to sound really dumb, but don't I know you? I remember you from somewhere.

—I saw you in here last night, she said. With a cute little redhead. Maybe you saw me.

—Maybe. I don't think so.

—I don't think so either. I recognized you too. We all recognize each other. But I haven't seen you at meetings. Still go?

Leverton smiled. So that was it. It was like something you carried around inside you that only those who carried the same thing could see. He looked at her. She had it. The fitness, the wellness, was like something she applied to her

84

illness, to deny it. It just giftwrapped it. The last couple of days had seen his own fancy giftwrap fall away from him in shreds.

—I haven't been to a meeting for fifteen years maybe, he said, looking at the vodka martini shine like jewelry bunched in silver satin. Lovelier than Lana Turner's hair. Than Cinderella's slipper. Than a starry, starry sky. Marcie reached a hand across and pinged the rim of his glass with her fingernail.

—So. Sure you want to do this?

He picked up his drink, felt the cold slip of the glass, heard the ice knock and chuckle, that beautiful sound. The cruelty of it: different in alcohol. Crazy but true. You could tell by the sound.

—*swirl.*

—Ken, she said, I can't let you do this. This is my responsibility. You know that. You do not do this. She held his wrist with one hand, took the glass with the other, signaled the barman. Larry? Can we get another club soda here?

—Thanks, Leverton said. But that's not the problem. But thanks anyway. It was just, I don't know.

She raised an eyebrow. I don't know? It never is the problem. Don't give me any shit, Ken. I've been there. I'm still there. We never ever leave, do we? So tell me about your day.

Leverton laughed, like a cough. My day? I'm going insane, hearing voices in my head, so my partners canned my ass. Changed the locks. I'm history. I'm a whale-watcher. A fine end to a distinguished career.

Marcie lit another cigarette. Zippo clink and spark, smell

of petrol. Walk away, she said, narrowing her eyes against the smoke. Look at something else. It's only work. You did that already.

Leverton examined her face. You do remind me of somebody, he said. A long time ago. The hair threw me.

—Going to tell me? Or do I arm-wrestle you for it?

—My wife.

—I remind you of your wife. Makes me think she's not your wife anymore, when you say that.

—I guess she's not. I'm sorry.

—You guess she's not? She either is or she isn't. Anyway. It's not like I was going to ask you to marry me. Tell me about the redhead.

—My business partner. Was my business partner.

—She the one that changed the locks?

—God, no. I wish she'd stop trying to help me, give me up. She should remember where her future is. Not with some crazy bum talking to the wiring.

—I've seen her here a couple times. Piece of work, that girl.

—Piece of work? Yeah. I think so. We have more in common all the time, don't we? said Leverton, sipping his club soda. He could taste the No Alcohol. Soft drink. Not a real drink. Like eating pictures out of recipe books and telling yourself it's food. Something stupid and smirking about a soft drink, like it thinks it's the real thing, like you actually really desire it. An ugly flirt, sticky with makeup.

—Hello again? Marcie said. Come back? Only don't apologize, okay? I may set fire to you. She snapped the Zippo under his nose.

—I was just thinking, he said.

—I know. Club soda. Sometimes just the smell of it makes

me sick to my stomach. So I'll get a Coke, and drink that until I realize I never really liked it. Or a Dr Pepper.

—Tab. Sprite. Fabulous drinks. We're drinking like children.

—Well, we showed that we can't be trusted, didn't we?

A woman opening the door from the street whistled between her teeth.

—I have to go. Gonna behave like a grown-up?

Leverton said, I guess. She kissed him on the cheek as she slid from her stool, and he saw the logo on her jacket. Ampar. Everything about the woman was familiar somehow. The barman called after her, Hey, this yours? He nodded at a shoebox on the end of the bar.

—God! she said. Thanks, Barry. I'll forget my head next. She picked up the box and turned to Leverton. Buy yourself a shave. Keep the lighter. A gift.

He warmed his club soda for maybe five minutes, feeling very tired and alone very suddenly. He picked up the Zippo, thumbed the lid open and shut. Familiar. That sound. Memories. Seeing faces underlit briefly. Sweating faces, eyes flicking. The crackle of grass, muffled crump of mortar off in the darkness.

—*love to fucking flame man and I . . . torched those motherfucking Charlie huts that was good shit the flames I love that fucking Son My shit man . . .*

He dropped the lighter in his pocket. Larry? he said. Barry? The barman looked up from his copy of *Guns & Ammo*. I'll get that vodka martini now?

Dean Mance, what a catch, thought Klein. What a so totally fortunate woman I am to be able to look at you across our lovely coffee table with a plate of cold food in your lap, talking to some movie guy about something that's never going to happen. What coupon did I get to clip for you? Why did God single me out for all this deep attention? Your mother was right, floppy-fringe. Go ahead, push your hair back, that's it. Laugh, show your big white teeth. There you go! Shake your cuff. Go on. You did it! I love the Dean Show! I could sit here all night and watch it. I do sit here all night and watch it. It's a re-run, but I can't get enough of it, apparently. I love the next bit, where you put the plate on the table, and I pick it up and take it into the kitchen and scrape the food into the trash. And I do it really loud so you look up during your call and frown at me! So I rattle the knife even louder! And you move to the balcony and pace up and down jingling your fucking coins in your pocket. Fuck it.

—Dean.

Mance held his hand flat up to her, kept talking. The hand said, Stop, I'm busy. Later. This is important. You're not. Said all those things.

—Dean.

The fingers on the hand crabbed into a claw, and Mance shook his head fiercely. This was a Big Moment, clearly. She raised her voice.

—We have to talk, Dean.

He held his hand over the mouthpiece, hissed at her. Kirby, for fuck's sake! Do I interrupt you at work? Do I? Thank you.

Without thinking, she stood and hurled herself bodily at him across the table, grabbed at the phone, shouting his name. She snapped the plate in his lap with her knee, dug her nails into his wrist. He pushed his hand under her jaw, tipping her head back. She twisted away, grabbed his hair and wrenched the phone from his hand as the couch tipped over. She was astride his chest as his head knocked on the parquet. A pot yucca teetered like a drunk from a revolving door, shivered upright, gently brushed Mance's face.

—Asshole! she yelled. Asshole! Talk to me, God damn it!

Mance was hyperventilating. Get . . . off . . . my . . . shirt, he croaked. My glasses, where's my . . .

Klein found his glasses, a little twisted, pushed them onto his face.

—Hear me better now? Hear me? Read my fucking teeth?

They froze like that for a second. A little voice came from the phone in Klein's fist.

—Oh, shit, hissed Mance. Turn the fucker off, Kirby. Press end.

—Believe me, Dean, pressing end is what I'm doing. I am so pressing end I broke my nail.

The phone beeped. They looked at it.

—Let me take it, Kirby. Let me take it. I'm begging with this.

Klein flicked her hair from her face, put the phone to her ear. I'm sorry, she said pleasantly, Dean cannot take your call right now as my foot is on his neck.

—Glad to hear it, Kirb, said her mother-in-law. It was you I needed to speak to anyway.

Mance flailed for the phone. It's for me, Klein snapped, and stood up, grinding her heel into his chest.

—Hi, Bobbie. I had to fight your son for the phone.

—And you won? He's no son of mine. Listen, sweetie, the cute guy you were with last night? He's here again, only he's not so cute. We have him in my office, but he's in a bad state, poor boy, and he's asking for you. Can you come by?

—You let him drink?

—Let him drink? It's a bar, Kirby.

—I'm on my way. No more drink, okay?

Her husband was groaning into a sitting position, picking shards of sticky plate from his lap. Klein dropped the phone on his head. It's all yours, handsome, she said. Your problem is, you can't read the writing on the wall even when it's your dinner.

Herrera's office was themed out like a goldrush bordello madame's room, ensuite bathroom full of Victorian plumbing and candles. Tiffany lamps, rugs, big pink painting of fat woman with fan, bar stocked with bourbon, the whole deal. And a bed in the corner behind a lace canopy, very feminine, ruched coverlet, frilly pillows, fringed valance. Leverton sprawled on it like a sidewalk suicide, arm twisted up behind his head somehow. One shoe was missing.

—Jesus, Klein said. Is he alive?

Herrera sat down at her desk, suddenly short of breath. She rubbed her eyes, and her voice was a little slurred. I've seen deader, believe me, she said. But not, I have to say, in my bed. They either get poured into a cab, or folded into a Rubbermaid. I hope he appreciates it.

—I appreciate it, Bobbie. You're a pal. Hey, are you okay?

Herrera smoothed her Botox eye with a gold fingernail. Yeah, she said, in a voice cracked with smoke. Just a little rundown or something, I don't know. Well, if he asks for me when he sobers up, tell him he's not my type, okay? But tell him thanks for asking.

Klein smiled at her. Quit that tart-with-a-heart shtick, Bobbie. This guy is nobody's type, believe me. What you see here is the beauty part.

—I'll be in the bar being fabulous if you need me, Herrera

said, using the arms of the chair to stand up. Look after him, Kirb.

Klein looked at Herrera. It looks like it's you who needs looking after, she said. Are you coming down with something?

Herrera waved a hand dismissively. Oh, I'll be fine, sweetie, she said, and Klein noticed the unsteadiness in her step as she left. She drew a chair up to the bed, pulled Leverton's arm out from behind his neck and laid it by his side. He grunted.

—Ken?

His right eye flickered open. Sick, he said thickly, going to . . .

Klein pulled back just in time. He lurched over the side of the bed and vomited noisily into a pair of lace slippers on a fluffy rug. She skipped into the bathroom, hearing him retch again through a groan, soaked a towel in the basin, wrung it out. She went back into the office and wrapped his face in the towel, rolled up the slippers in the rug and put the bundle under the shower in the bath.

Leverton sat on the edge of the bed, holding the towel to his face.

—Going to run that by me again? she said, standing with her hands on her hips.

He mumbled something, could have been No. Klein went back into the bathroom, found the air freshener, squirted it around the office. Then she cleaned up the rug and the slippers as best she could and rinsed the bath out with some toilet cleanser. Then she washed her hands and went back to see how Leverton was. He was sitting up on the bed, looking like a sack of shit.

—Can you stand up? she said. Can you walk?

He wiped the towel down his face and looked at her. I'm sorry, Kirb.

—Yeah, she said. You're sorry. So that's okay. Go wash up and I'll drive you home. If you can bear to, take a shower. For me, okay?

—Shave, he slurred, holding a chairback as if it were a Zimmerframe.

—Forget the shave, we're not kissing. Just shower, okay? Go on, get in there. I'll get you a coffee.

Leverton laughed, no pleasure in it. None of this, he said, pantomime sober, is particularly funny.

—Shower, Klein said, taking his arm and guiding him through the bathroom door. No rush. Take as long as it takes, okay?

She waited until she heard the water start and turned to go into the lounge, noticed a photograph by the door for the first time, hung low down, half hidden behind a fern. She leaned to look at it, separating the fern fronds. It was Dean, of course, as a little boy, that had caught her eye. That floppy fringe, big smile. He was standing in the background with an older boy, his mother in a headscarf and sunglasses in the foreground, hugging a toy donkey and mugging a surprised look for the camera. This other boy. Klein knew him, even out of focus. She'd looked at his face a lot recently. She unhooked the picture from the wall and held it under a lamp to get a better view. Her eyes narrowed in certainty, and she tapped the glass over the young man's chest. She hung the picture back on the wall and whispered, Hello there, Bradley.

Bobbie Herrera was at the center of a group of laughing men in the lounge, draping herself around somebody's shoulders.

Klein watched her at work for a while, then caught her eye
– the good one – with a wave. Herrera made an excuse,
kissed a few cheeks, wobbled over.

—How is he?

—In the shower. I think he ruined your slippers. And a
rug. I tried to clean up in there.

Herrera shook her head. Don't give it another thought,
sweetie. He could use a coffee?

—We all could. Give him a few minutes. Listen, can I ask
you something?

Herrera sat on a leather couch, the slit in her skirt showing
a stocking top, patted the cushion beside her. She fanned her
face with her hand. Hot in here, she said. Is this about Dean?

Klein sat next to her. It's not Dean, she said. It's about
Bradley Brewster. The picture in your office. You with the
toy donkey? That is Brewster with Dean, isn't it?

Herrera's smile stiffened. What about him?

—Some years back Brewster approached Dean to be his
agent, but I had no idea they knew each other as boys. He
never mentioned it, and I don't understand why.

Herrera said nothing, but put a hand to her mouth, like
she was checking for the smile that was no longer there.

—Bobbie?

—Not right now, sweetie, she said. Not right now. I'll get
those coffees.

She patted Klein's knee and stood up, moving away
through the press of bodies. Her place was taken almost
immediately by a guy whose tan was the same color as his
suit and his ponytail. Hey there, he said. Paul French. Don't
I know you? He pointed at her with the damp end of his
cigar.

—As well as you're ever going to, Klein said, watching the cheap charm drain from his face like dirty water.

Leverton said nothing all the way back to his house, just sat rigidly staring straight ahead with his hands gripping his thighs, gathering the legs of his pants into hot wet creases. Klein tried one or two openers, gave up. He didn't look dead anymore, so that was an improvement. His mouth worked up and down from time to time. When Klein swung the Porsche into the driveway and doused the lights he turned his head to her and whispered one word, his face a frown. Counting, he said. She got out the car and went around to open his door, saw the front door of his house was open. Leverton stood for a while, leaning on the targa top briefly.

—Are you okay? Klein said.

—Why do you keep asking me if I'm okay? he said. I'm not okay. He sucked in a lungful of cool night air. I may never be okay again. Thanks for all this, Kirb, all this . . .

—I'm staying here tonight, she said. You're not safe on your own. Tomorrow we'll get you some help. You leave your house open?

—Luck, he said. Left the keys in my car.

Inside, Klein turned on the lights, seeing Leverton wince against the brightness. She looked around, said, This minimal approach, kind of hard to tell if anything's been stolen, isn't it?

—Only the stuff I treasured, he said. The quiet. The calm. They took all that.

—We're going to get you to bed, Ken. You'll feel better in the morning.

94

—Kirby, I'll never feel better again. Everything I had is gone.

—Trying to depress me? It's working. Don't push your luck here.

Leverton held her shoulders, looked into her eyes. Kirb, you can't help me. I can't let you think you can, okay? You have to walk away, look at something else. I don't want to be responsible for dragging you down with me, don't do that to me. I couldn't stand it. Go home to your husband. This is not your problem.

Klein said, Bed. I'll take the spare room.

—I've slept in the spare room for twenty years. I'll take the couch.

She couldn't stop her eyes drifting to the sealed-up door, knew she'd said a stupid thing. I'm fine on the couch, she said.

—I'm not sleepy, he said.

—Go to bed, she said.

—Talk to me. Turn out the lights and talk to me.

—Your clothes smell, Ken. Go to bed. I'm tired.

—If I get changed, will you talk to me?

—I'll see if there's anything to eat. As if.

Leverton walked across the room, only a little unsteadiness there. They hadn't found his shoe. Crumpled old guy, walking with one shoe. He stopped at the fireplace, took something bright from his pocket and put it on the slate shelf. When he'd gone to his room Klein went to have a look at it. Old Zippo lighter with a mildly pornographic picture on it. Crude engraving on the back, worn smooth. 'Ken L. Cant Go To Hell When Your Already There'. She'd never figured the guy for a Vietnam sentimentalist. She shook her head, went into the kitchen, grilled some goat's cheese, ate it with toast. Leverton didn't show, so she peeked into his room. He was collapsed in bed, clothes half off. She made sure she could hear his breathing, and shut the door gently. In the hallway she pressed her hand against the sealed-up door. It didn't give. She ran her fingers over the barely discernible patch left by the handle. What goes on in this house? What? She found a sheet in a closet and made up a bed on the couch. The room chalk-pale in the light diffused by the window blinds. Everything gray, colorless as beach glass. She stripped to her underwear, slipped under the sheet. This drab gauze covering the wound of color. Or the nature of things, revealed without the paint of day. The contradiction of moonlight; this insubstantiality is the substance. No depth, no distance in the scenery of dream, everywhere is in between. Memory reduced to dust. She closed her eyes. Perhaps a police siren somewhere, then the gray caul of silence. The color of sleep, of ghosts. Dust.

Still Feel Smart?

Next morning, when Klein had told him some kind of care program was looking inevitable, Leverton told her about The Garden. She'd made some calls, watching him packing through his bedroom door. She found it strangely touching. This beat-up guy taking clean shirts from a drawer, making space for his washbag, like he was preparing for a holiday or something. Occasionally his shoulders would slump, and his head droop, as he leaned on the suitcase or the bedhead, as if he was trying to remember what he had to do next.

She looked at him now, sitting in the passenger seat of the Porsche with his hands clasped in his lap, as she took the turn off Mulholland Drive.

—You sure this is it? she said.

The Garden didn't look like a care center. No white coats, no corridors. An informal community of redwood bungalows high in the Hollywood hills, surrounded by parkland. Established in the sixties to discreetly dry out movie stars, it now catered to anyone who needed a retreat and could keep off medication. The rule was simple: no drugs of any kind, in your pocket or your bloodstream. There was a kind of Zen discipline, a routine of simple things, that Leverton appreciated twenty years before, and had kept with him.

After the brutal hospital detox it had seemed like some kind of heaven. The place hadn't changed at all.

—This is it, he said.

They pulled up in front of the reception building. A young man in denims and a white tee came down the steps.

—Hi. I'm Matt, he said. You've been with us before, Ken?

There was a long pause before Leverton spoke. A while back, he said.

They stood on the steps. Leverton gazed unseeingly at the raw skingraft of LA peeled out far below. The air was full of the smell of warm leaves. Klein, standing a step or two below him, and seeming almost the height of a child to him, reached up and held his hand.

—You'll be okay? she said.

He looked at her in a brilliant and terrible instant of lucidity. No, he thought, he wasn't okay; he would never be okay again. But more than that, he felt something surge up and open inside him, something that caused him so much sudden physical pain his legs gave way beneath him and he fell heavily to the steps. Matt leaned over and supported him, holding his shoulders, and Klein stumbled on the bottom step as she reached for him, spilling her purse.

—I'm okay, he said, with what remained of his breath. In a silence that seemed at once infinitely long and yet without duration, Leverton understood what he felt. This was it; an unexpected and overwhelming access of feeling, at once clarifying yet complicating. In that moment, when their eyes met, and he felt the inexpressibly delicate touch of her hand in his, that little heartbreaking hand, he knew he was too late for Kirby Klein, that he should have been in love with her, forever, and that his love had been denied, unspoken, and was now a thing of memory, just dust. The voices that brought him here had rushed into the measureless void left by love inside him, and filled it with babble, echoing mad babble. The voices were in his heart, not his head. He saw her eyes through his tears and his hands went up to his face, unable to withstand her kindness, a concern as unassailable as his loss, and as unwanted.

Matt unclipped his beeper from his belt. You'll be fine, he said. I'll just get some help here and we'll get you to your room. Take it easy, okay?

Klein looked at Leverton, hunched and almost fetal with a pain she couldn't begin to understand.

—Take care, Ken.

Leverton opened his fingers wide enough to look at her. She saw him blink, a prisoner, and she saw the silver scar at his temple, like a signature.

Curtis Maitland refilled Amity's glass with Krug and looked around the room. Still no Kirby Klein. She'd show. Everybody else had, except for Leverton, of course. Klein had called to tell him she'd got Ken into The Garden. Until he felt better. Maitland said the company's insurance would carry it. He'd looked after him before, he'd do it again. People were asking about him, of course. Maitland told them it was overwork. Tara Van Zandt had been unusually concerned. He'd done his best to reassure her that her account was receiving his and Peter's immediate personal attention. Maitland hated fighting fires. He preferred to cut the trees down before they caught light.

Still. It was a good party. The doors to the deck had been removed, and it was a beautiful late afternoon. Consuela was dressed like a French maid, and the guys from the catering service swung by with trays of caviar on Ritz crackers. The entire MLA payroll was there, filling the large room. Peter Reitz had brought a tall blonde in a scrap of clothing like something blown up against her, and Maitland had held her eye and her hand exactly long enough. Reitz was a star turn today, smiling like he'd crack his head open. Maitland watched how the blonde's dress clung to the hollow of her ass cheek, like it was damp. She turned her head, saw him looking at her across the room, as if he'd called her name. Judy. He didn't smile at her. Never smile, don't blink, focus on one eye, visualize the act, think the word. She dropped her gaze to her glass, pretended to laugh at something Reitz had said.

A short while later, Maitland found himself standing next to her on the deck. That meticulously choreographed hive-dance of parties. He looked at her. That look, that hook, was all the more barbed for being closer, the lure that much brighter.

—You have a beautiful house, she said, holding his gaze this time.

—Thank you. It's an appropriate context for beautiful people. Is that an Alaia?

She dropped her head slightly so her eyes were shaded by a fall of honey-colored hair.

—I'm impressed. Not many guys I know would know that.

—Not many women I know could wear his work. It takes definition. Your body has beautiful definition.

—Thank you. Ah . . . am I being hit on by my date's boss, by any chance?

Maitland smiled at the phrase, and the image it held for him.

100

—Would you like to be?

Her eyes widened with her smile. Austin interrupted with a hand on his arm. Curtis, he said, Kirby's here. Maitland held up a champagne bottle and tapped it with a fork. There was almost immediate quiet, and a respectful semicircle formed for him. Somebody laughing off in a corner was hushed. Maitland noticed Klein standing on her own at the door, looking sensational in black. He waited a second, spoke.

—People, he said. Welcome. It's good to see so many happy faces here. It's a very special time for us at MLA, and we're here to celebrate a couple of new beginnings for us. Now I know we all wish Ken were here to share our achievements, and I'm sure you join with me now in extending to him our best wishes for a quick and full recovery. He wants us to be the moment as it happens, and sends his love to you all.

There was a round of applause for this sentiment. Klein, taking a canapé from a silver tray, didn't join in. She doubted if Maitland had spoken with Leverton. Be the moment? Sends his love? Yeah, right. Ken had more class. She heard Maitland's voice fill the room easily, without volume. He had that tone somehow.

—We're here tonight to honor a new partner. It's a rare event . . .

Klein blocked this stuff out. Peter Reitz. Jesus. She knew he'd never forgiven her coming in over his head. A phrase Maitland spoke caught her attention.

—Winning the TasteLicious account was a powerful team achievement.

Klein took a deep breath through her clenched teeth. Team achievement? She felt her face flush with anger.

Maitland had his arm around Peter's shoulders. Enough, she thought. Enough. She stepped back through the doorway, walked down the hallway trying to order her thoughts. A surge of laughter and applause made her bite her lip. She went into the garden and slammed the door behind her, stood on the steps a while calming herself down.

—Not enjoying the party?

The voice made her start. Shanna, wearing just a pink translucent sun visor and body oil, sitting by the pool, toes in the water. She waved a joint in a silver holder. You need to relax, she said. Like a little?

Klein said, No, thanks. Isn't there a dress code here?

Shanna flicked the brim of her visor. You're looking at it, honey. Ha ha. Funny girl. So. Who's the party for?

Klein looked at her watch for something to do. I was kind of slow on that one, she said.

—That's Curtis, Shanna said. Full of surprises. Quite the party guy. A clown on fire. Ha ha. Come sit with me.

Klein watched as Shanna took a long suck on the joint and reclined on her towel. All-over tan, and no body hair at all. Klein said, Tell me something. You and Curtis. What kind of marriage is this?

Shanna chuckled, stubbed out the joint on a damp tile. Crazy bastard, she said, her voice papery from the smoke. Bastard. It's kind of like, ooh, Shanna is his pet tiger! Out here in the jungle! Shanna, queen of the jungle! He feeds me things.

Klein moved to a lounger next to Shanna and sat down. What does he feed you, Shanna?

Shanna growled, stretched, beads of sweat spangling her flat golden stomach. Anything his wild little pussy wants, she

102

said, smiling down at her breasts. Juicy young boys. Men, and – she paused before whispering the word – girls.

—Challenging bourgeois mores, said Klein in a bored drawl. Barbie invites Ken and Sindy into her lovely home.

Shanna snickered. Wanna swim?

—Hardly.

Shanna shrugged, as if it was Klein's loss. Well, she said, brightening suddenly, come inside and look at my gallery. You'll be surprised, Shanna guarantees.

—You know that referring to yourself in the disassociated third person is a sign of dysfunction?

—You could be right. But you really need to loosen up, honey. Come look at my pictures. More fun than in there.

She took Klein's hand. Klein glanced back at the house. Couldn't see it through the bushes from here. She let herself be led along the path to the guest cottage at the far end of the pool. Shanna's animal ease with her own naked body made Klein feel suddenly and awkwardly overdressed. The white, flat-roofed bungalow was reached by a Japanese-style lacquered wooden bridge over a narrow channel in the swimming pool. Klein could see inside through the uninterrupted glass wall, just like the open elevation to a dollhouse. Shanna slid the door to the living room and drew her inside, still holding her hand. The airconditioning was a shock after the oven heat of the garden. Shanna shivered pleasurably.

—I love this, she giggled. Look! She let go of Klein's hand and offered up her breast. See how hard my nipples go? It's like they're thermometers or something!

—I knew you had to be useful for something, Klein said quietly, looking around the room. It was surprisingly tasteful for somebody with rainbow toenails. Pale-blue color-washed walls. Painted Provençal furniture, comfortable chairs, an open fireplace full of unburned tallow candles. Klein nodded at the far wall, crowded with photographs. That your gallery?

—Uh huh. It's fun!

Klein folded her arms and walked across the room, conscious of Shanna's eyes on her. She made a detour to the fireplace, attracted by something she recognized in a niche in the stone chimney. MLA had quite a few examples of that particular award. A fat gold pencil on a chrome base, tarnished and dusty, the engraving obscured with corrosion. She rubbed it with her thumbnail. Best Art Direction for a Press Campaign, 1974. Ken Leverton. She was seeing his name written all over the place. In the strangest places. She turned to Shanna, pointed to the award.

—Why do you have this?

Shanna shrugged. Curtis leaves some of his stuff here. That wooden Indian over there is his too. So what? Check out my pictures!

Most of the photographs were portraits, taken by the pool, and a good few of them Klein recognized from the party pages of celebrity magazines at her hairdresser's. C-list lens dogs from daytime TV, poodle-hair rock stars, disgraced basketball players with their eyes up in their head and their tongues lolling. Kind of people who pay to be stalked. Some were signed, in the distressingly childish fake-artistic flourish affected by the self-important and illiterate. There were a few shots seemingly taken with a telephoto lens through the bedroom window, of Shanna and whomever in bed. Some of her partners were unrecognizable from the backs of their heads, and Shanna was pleased to tell Klein their names.

—This is Tischia Burke White? She is a doll!

—Never heard of her. I know this one, though, Klein

said, pointing to a bare hook in a gap between pictures. The invisible man, right?

—You're funny! The invisible man! Might as well be. Curtis took him away. He's dead anyway.

Klein frowned at her. Dead? Who's the dead guy, Shanna?

Maitland held up his hand to silence the applause. I want you all to just kick back and relax tonight, he said. There'll be a barbecue on the beach in an hour or so, so don't spoil your burger appetite on caviar. Enjoy!

A jazz trio in the corner slipped into a breezy bossa and Maitland moved off through the crowd, placing his hand on the occasional shoulder and sharing a word or two here and there. He found Consuela in the kitchen, whispered something, sprang upstairs to the back of the house, his private bathroom. Two minutes later, Consuela came in, carrying an imported glass bottle of Evian, and turned the lock behind her. A hook of thick black hair fell from her lace cap and stuck to her lip. He took the bottle. Ice cold.

—Keep your hands behind your back, he said, his face suddenly dark. She leaned back against the door, her eyes glittering. He put the bottle on the side of the tub and put his hands on her breasts, the little white apron rustling against the stiff black cotton dress. He moved his hands, feeling the texture of her brassiere through her uniform.

—Tell me what you want, he said, his voice low and soft.

—I want you to hurt me, she responded automatically, her mouth contorting in something like a smile, her voice an expressionless whisper. He pinched the points of her breasts. Her eyes closed and she sighed. He squeezed harder, biting his lower lip, eyes narrowing. She winced and let out a little cry of pain. He balled his right hand into a fist and punched her in the belly as her legs collapsed under her, and she splayed to the floor. He looked at her breast heaving, heard her breath quickening, pressed the toe of his shoe up into her crotch.

—Stand up, he said. He slid the thin Italian belt from his waist and wrapped it around his fist. Consuela pushed herself back up the tiled wall, hands flat against it. Maitland listened to her moan, saw her eyelids flutter. He leaned close to her face, whispered, I love you. He paused. Bitch, he said, the word sharp as a bite. She shook. I love you, he said, tenderly as a father. Bitch, he spat. I love you. Bitch. He snapped the end of the belt across her breasts. I love you. He grabbed the hair at the back of her head, curled it in his fist, pulling her head back. Bitch. He spat in her open mouth, looped the belt around her neck. I love you. Pulled it tight, pushing his forearm up under her chin. Bitch. His cock was out. He pulled her panties up between her ass. I love you. He pushed himself up inside her. Wet, hot, tight. What do you want? What does my little fucking bitch want? Hurt me, she said, barely audible. He hit the side of her face with the flat of his hand, pushed her off him, onto the floor, bent to crush her face flat against the tiles and fold her skirt up over her back. He slipped the belt from her neck and whipped her bared ass twice, forehand and backhand. She yelped. The olive skin over the hollowing muscle. He knelt behind her, pulled her head back by her hair, tilted her hips up and pushed himself up her ass, feeling the damp lace twist of her panties against his cock. She moaned. He reached for a towel and wrapped it around her head, coiling it up at the back. Bitch. I love you. Bitch. I love you. He pressed his hand against the small of her back, pushed her flat against the floor, forced himself right up inside her, twisted the towel tighter around her face, hit her head against the side of the tub. I love you. Bitch.

The calmness came over him, and he lay still, feeling her ass muscles spasm, relax. He unwrapped the towel from her head, stroked her hair back from her face. I love you. He kissed her cheek. My little fucking slut. My piece of shit. He pulled himself from her ass, slowly, feeling the head of his cock tug against the rim of muscle, and turned her over. He took the glass bottle from the edge of the tub and pulled off the top, kneeling between her legs. She began to say something, so he pushed her jaw shut with his hand. Shut the fuck up. He dribbled some water down over her cunt. Like that? Like that? He tilted the bottle, worked the neck up between her wet lips, spilling water up into her. Pushed it up a little further. I know what you like.

She was whimpering now, almost like a little song, with a melody to it. He pulled the bottle out, shook water into her face. Pushed the neck between his fingers into her mouth. Suck. He slid his cock up inside her, delicious slippery cold for a second or two. Suck. Come for me. Going to come for me? Her fingers linked behind his head, the bottle fell away, and she pressed his face to hers, spat the cold water into his mouth, bit his lip. His hands went to her throat, squeezed, until she went limp and heavy in his arms, and her eyes rolled up in her head. He came. You okay?

Her eyes opened, and she smiled up at him, that smile like a drug, a dream. I love you, she said. Bitch, he said, and kissed her eyes, breathing in her smell, like the interior of a church on a hot day, and he felt himself get hard again inside her.

★

Shanna's voice was a complaint. Excuse me? she said, this is depressing me up? He was in the papers a while back, I don't know. Brad. Bradley! You know.

Klein's mouth went dry. She almost whispered the name. Bradley Brewster?

Shanna put an arm around Klein's waist, and pulled her up against her hip. She smiled. Ever been masturbated by a woman?

Klein elbowed her away. You're getting tan oil on my suit, she said. Shanna, this is important. Listen to me. You knew Bradley Brewster? And Curtis took his photograph?

Shanna pirouetted woozily, her arms linked above her head. She half sang, Curtis took everyone's photograph, he takes everyone's picture. He's a por . . . a photographer.

Klein watched her dance into the bedroom, followed her. I don't mean that, she said. Why did Curtis remove his picture, Shanna?

Shanna fell onto the bed, grabbing Klein's wrist and pulling her down on top of her. For a second their lips touched. Klein pulled free, furious.

—Oh, stop it, Shanna, for fuck's sake. Grow up.

Shanna rolled onto her side, pointed up out of the window. Welcome to the gallery, she smiled. Klein stood and looked where she was pointing, above the shrubbery at the end of the pool, to the balcony on the second floor, a shadow, a glint of something.

She looked down at Shanna on the bed. Eyes half closed, hands on her breasts.

—You stupid . . .

Making a sudden decision never to waste another word on the woman, Klein went into the living room, snatched up Leverton's award, strode back up the garden to the house,

108

stopped with her hand on the door. Inside, voices getting closer. No way she felt like socializing right now. Nobody here she wanted to talk to. She turned and strode down the steps and through the garage, dragging the sharp point of the award in a vicious scrawl along the side of Shanna's Pontiac. Last to arrive, Klein's Porsche was the only car not blocked in the driveway. She spun the wheels on the gravel and screamed in reverse down to the road. There she stopped, while her heart slowed. Don't drive mad, Kirby, she said. And don't use the disassociated third person. And talking to yourself is for crazy guys.

She found her cigarettes and her mobile phone in the glove compartment and checked her hair in the mirror. The phone beeped. It was her husband.

—Where the fuck have you been, Kirby?

Klein put the car into gear and stuck a cigarette in her mouth. Why? she said. You miss me like a crazy boy?

—My mother is in hospital. My mother is dying. Still feel smart?

Perfect

He'd forgotten Venice. The suitcase hadn't.

—*Casa Del Sogno. The Borsa. Motoscafo from the airport. Cold. Spray from the lagoon. Laughter.*

—That was Sonia.

First time he'd spoken her name for, how long? They'd stood in the stern of the motoscafo, leaning on the roof of the cabin, all the way across the lagoon, watching Venice coalesce from the mist like a conjuring trick. How could he have forgotten? He sat on the edge of the futon in his room and looked at the battered leather suitcase. He formed the words in his mouth without speaking them, spelling the sound in his head.

—Where else? Where else did we go?

—*London. Paris. Rome. I went to Hawaii without you on the way back. I was crushed and dropped so many times. You'd be surprised at the stories you hear in the hold. Really.*

Leverton tuned out. He didn't want to hear about being slid under beds, thrown on top of wardrobes. London. Paris. Rome. Venice. He had been ill even then, he knew. Drinking all the way on the plane. A pint of vodka in the room. A kind of desperate fun, a last fling maybe, knowing in his heart it was over, scared to death to admit it. When he could still make her laugh. Funny how you start by making them laugh and finish by making them cry. Europe had been one long headache of bad laughter, that ugly sound you make when things really aren't funny anymore. He remembered pissing up against St Mark's Basilica, puking up in a restaurant somewhere, in his own lap. That had been the last time, before the laughter stopped. Even on the way back, that terrible fight when they'd lost the luggage. He'd stood swaying in the baggage reclaim at LAX, the cruelty coming out at last, the bitter dregs of their black dog days, cursing her until she huddled in a crouch, hands over her head, and cried and cried and cried. And he'd stood there and gloated. Very good. Very nice.

—Ken?

He looked up. An older guy. Jeans, sweatshirt with The Garden logo. Gray hair trimmed to stubble. Thin, too, moved like machinery. Steel-gray eyes.

—You don't remember me, do you?

Leverton blinked. No, he didn't. I'm sorry, he said.

—It's okay. Bryce Fuller? We changed a lot over the years.

—Jesus, Bryce . . . said Leverton, struggling to get up, his knees locked. Fuller put a hand on his shoulder.

—Don't get up. I'm coming down.

He sat next to Leverton and looked at him, his eyes flicking over Leverton's face, taking in all the new stuff. The new old stuff.

—Been a long time, he said. Didn't really expect to see you again. Don't know if I'm glad or what.

Leverton gripped his hand. Couldn't think of anything to say.

They looked at each other for a moment. Fuller saw Leverton's eyes go dead and slide away.

—Your room okay? he said. Leverton twitched, looked over his shoulder, like someone tapped him on it.

—Ken? Fuller waited, then turned to where Matt stood in the doorway, his arms folded across his chest. Matt, he said softly, I'll be here for a while, I think. No calls.

He watched Leverton's head tilt, like a satellite dish picking up signals from somewhere. Fuller had been an intern here the first time he'd met Leverton. Remembered a gaunt, pale guy with a heavy beard and shoulder-length hair. Leverton had just spent two months in intensive care, four more at a clinic, and was determined to get off the meds. Fuller had been assigned to him on a twenty-four-hour basis. It had been hard work, but rewarding. In truth, when clients came through the gates of The Garden they'd either been on the way to recovery or not desperately ill in the first place, which accounted for the enviable success rate and miracle cure reputation. Fuller had since done well at The Garden, and after a couple of years on a recent sabbatical, working with the terminally ill at a hospice in England, he had returned as Director with a different agenda. The vanity cure aspect was cut. They no longer accepted the bored and the hypochondriac. Medical references were insisted upon. A funded care program for those who couldn't afford it was seamlessly incorporated into the structure. The reputation of a country club for the mildly eccentric was replaced by an ethos of hard work and real improvement. But Fuller hated repeat customers. Especially this one. He'd taken a huge pride in his role in Leverton's recovery. And here he was, this thousand-year-old guy with the thousand-yard stare, back again. Fuller got to his feet.

—Ken, he said, we're going to take a walk. Let's take a walk.

Leverton stood up. No problem, he said. I'm here. Yes.

From the steps of the cabin a bark-chip path wound through glossily vivid clumps of rhododendron and jacaranda, between broadleaf trees enameling the grass with shifting scales of sunlight. People walked in couples or sat in groups. It was quiet, and yet the feeling of work being done was palpable. Nobody played ball or jogged or played music or ate food. No laughter.

—Remember how we work here? Fuller said. We ask pretty basic questions, pretty straight stuff, and you either answer honestly as you can, or not at all. And no pills. And you do the routine. You help with the food and you clean your room.

Leverton remembered nothing. This was just scenery to him. I remember, he said. He remembered Kirby Klein's eyes.

—Okay. Tell me about your wife, Ken.

—My wife? Oh, Sonia. Why? Okay. Not much to tell. She never came back.

—She went back to her family?

—No family to go back to. She's in Canada, doing okay.

—So you're legally separated, or divorced, or what?

—She left me, and I never got in touch. Nor she with me. Some pieces of paper you don't need to sign. I never wanted to marry again, and I guess she didn't either. I don't know. We just never got together to resolve it one way or the other. I still get her Talbot's catalogs in the mail.

They passed a woman doing tai chi, intently self-absorbed.

—And your work? The agency? Still with that est guy?

—Curtis. Curtis Maitland. We did good. I've been trying to retire, I guess. Hanging around getting in the way. Couldn't let go.

Leverton went through it all again. It seemed like telling

somebody else's story that had happened a long time ago. He was thinking about Kirby Klein. He was thinking about her all the time, he realized. He stopped in mid-sentence, forgot what he was saying. Fuller gave him a minute to continue before he spoke.

—So, he said, why now? What's the trigger?

They stopped by a rockpool surrounded by ferns. Beats me, Leverton said, watching the fish gleam in the pewter-colored water, thinking how strange it is, all this stuff coming to the surface, what goes on down there. Like the skin had peeled away; everything was like a metaphor, everything a sign or a signature, or a symbol. Stuff he had to understand. Revealed yet hidden. Stuff he couldn't read. He started crying, for no reason he knew, stood there for a while with the tears coming down his cheeks, Bryce's hand resting on his shoulder. That huge gulf wave of bleak loneliness. They stood together until he stopped crying. He wiped his eyes on his sleeve.

—Bryce, he said. I can't remember if there was something that triggered it or not. I can't remember the first time it happened. I can't remember a damn thing these days, not a damn thing. And the voices crowd in, and the memories crowd out. This is good, though. This is quiet. Trees and rocks and stuff. I don't get any shit from these guys. There was a whole lot of noise back in the cabin that threw me. Hard making out your voice.

—You can change rooms. I'll have Matt show you the possibilities.

—Are they wired up or something?

—Wired up? Intercom. Airconditioning. Power. Light. Maybe other services down there, I don't know. Is that what you mean?

114

—Can I sleep out here? Got a sleeping-bag?

Fuller squeezed Leverton's shoulder, feeling the tension there. Ken, you can sleep on the roof, in the pool, wherever you like. Whatever it takes to get you quiet again. Right now, you take a sauna, a massage, and get that check-up with our doctor, Pete Ross. I don't want to pre-empt anything here, but I don't want you to be negative about this voices thing. You're not drinking at all? Okay. Apart from that. So I guess you're just getting some kind of temporary flashback, and we will get through it. You don't seem physically ill to me. I can kind of smell that, you know? These things happen sometimes, and we get through them. It's not dying, Ken, it's living.

Leverton performed a little smile that convinced neither of them. He was tempted to do some kind of trick like he'd done for Klein, maybe with Fuller's watch, to show that he really was tapping into something outside of him. It would look like a trick, of course. It would look pathetic. He could recount what the suitcase had said to him on the steps, when Klein had said something he didn't hear and had driven away. He remembered her eyes, sad, gentle, beautiful eyes that she hid because they were the way into her, a way that everyone fell. She'd taken off her sunglasses and looked at him in a strange way. Before, she'd looked at him with liking, with respect, on occasion with admiration. Recently she'd looked at him with anxiety, surprise, and puzzlement. And sympathy. But this had been a new look, today, when she'd left. She'd been looking into him, and he hadn't been there for her. He couldn't return the look.

Bryce Fuller was speaking to him. He heard the sound of his voice. That look of Kirby's, he could easily fool himself it had been love. He could think himself into the logic of that. He could convince himself. Flatter himself. He tried to remember Tara's eyes, her look. No, that was an ad he remembered. He didn't know what color Tara's eyes were. Kirby's eyes were . . .

—Ken?

Leverton heard the name. His name. Oh, he said. I'm sorry. It's the quiet. Just thinking. Not listening at all. I'm sorry. He nodded down to the pool. I had a couple nice skeleton carp, he said. Floated up dead. Makes me wonder what kind of work they had to do to stay down there. Maybe they'd call that living. I don't know.

Dean Mance was in the corridor outside Bobbie Herrera's room, with his hand in his hair. He stared at Klein as she got out of the elevator, didn't go to meet her.

—How is she? Klein said, moving aside for a gurney.

—They're in there with her. Where the hell were you last night?

—I'm trying to think how you possibly noticed I'd gone, she said. But it doesn't matter. What happened here?

Mance pushed his hands into his pants pockets and jingled his loose change. There's something we have to talk about.

Klein took off her sunglasses. Go ahead.

—Did Mom ever talk to you about insurance?

—What? What are you talking about?

—This is costing me a fucking fortune. I can't find any medical insurance. There is no fucking insurance to cover this. Did she tell you she was insured?

Klein's mouth fell open in disbelief, her shoulders slumping.

116

—Bobbie is in there dying and you're asking me this?

Mance closed his eyes. Forget it, he said.

—So what happened, Dean? Tell me what happened, for Christ's sake.

—What's to tell? Barry found her this morning when he opened the club. But not until around noon, when he had to go into her office for something. She was lying on the floor, couldn't move. Couldn't breathe. He called the paramedics, got hold of me and I came here as soon as I could. Here I am. There she is. Here you are, you know?

A doctor came out of the room. He looked at Mance, then Klein.

—You're both related to Miss Herrera?

—Kirby Klein. Bobbie is my mother-in-law. What's happening? How is she?

He looked at Mance. You haven't told her?

—Just about the insurance aspect, Klein said.

—Okay. Your mother-in-law is in a critical condition, and we're doing what we can. There is respiratory trauma and she's in partial paralysis. The prognosis is not that good. I'm sorry.

Klein said, Can we see her? What happened here?

—You can go in as soon as the nurse finishes up. I'm afraid she won't know you're here. Mrs Klein, can you tell me if she was taking any prescribed medication to your knowledge, or under any kind of medical treatment, or was taking any prohibited drugs? This is very important.

Klein thought hard. She was fine, she said. The occasional migraine, but . . . wait a minute. She was having that Botox treatment?

The doctor looked blank.

—Shit, said Mance, the coin jingle suddenly stopping. Botox. I forgot that stuff. Damn. The facelift stuff.

Klein felt like hell. The same stuff that gives you botulism, she said.

The doctor looked down at the chart, at his notes. Well, he said, I need to confer, but it looks like Miss Herrera may have symptoms concomitant with that. I'd ask you not to go in just yet?

He went back into Herrera's room and shut the door. Mance walked to the window and glared out over the parking lot, moving his jaw with his hand. Jesus Christ, he said. Symptoms concomitant with botulism? We find that guy, we sue his ass with the biggest malpractice suit he'll ever see.

Klein was remembering something Bobbie had said, a couple of weeks back. Some joke about mainlining the stuff, now she didn't have to go retail. Some joke. She looked at her husband. He wasn't looking at her. She didn't recognize him as the guy she'd married. Husband, she thought. What a stupid word. What a stupid thing. To think she'd invested sympathy in the guy on the way over to the hospital. He'd need support, she'd told herself. He'd be hurting. But she hadn't expected him to be hurting with the prospect of paying the hospital bill and suing people. Maybe it was his way of dealing with the situation, deflecting his emotions so he didn't have to confront the truth of his dying mother. Maybe. She went to him and put her hand on his arm. His mobile beeped in his suit pocket. Her hand fell away as he put the phone to his ear.

—Certainly I'll take the call, Sandi, he said. You're breaking up. I'm trying for a better signal right now.

118

He moved down the corridor, bending toward the window, turning this way and that, trying to improve the reception. Klein watched his features freeze into his phone face. Big fucking shit-eating grin. Oh yes, she recognized him now okay. That tall guy down there, the good-looking guy with the floppy fringe, taking the important call. That was her husband. The guy she hated most in all the whole wide world.

A man and a woman in whites went quickly past her into Bobbie's room, moving her aside with the briefest of looks. A light over the door was flashing red. After a minute or so it stopped flashing. From somewhere down the corridor she heard Mance's laugh.

Kirby Klein clenched her fists and bit her lip to stop the tears. She felt stupidly alone. Every door was shut. Every back was turned. She stared at her shoes, her little patent pumps. A stupid tear splashed against a shiny toe. She wiped her eye with the back of her hand, feeling foolish, feeling wretched and weak. And then she felt all this confusion and sadness and mess coalesce into something she could begin to handle, to understand, to use. Anger.

He'd tried to help in the kitchen, be busy like the rest of them there. Beautiful big sunny room, normal room. Herbs and dried flowers hung from redwood roof beams. Be normal. He guessed that was what they all did there, make this effort to do the normal stuff, prepare salads, vegetables, move plates about. Talk. He was no different. They were all making this heroic effort to just look normal together. A guy who couldn't stop crying for more than a minute at a time was cutting bread at the long refectory table under the window. He'd wipe his eyes with the back of his hand, look

119

about embarrassedly, say I'm okay, really, I'm good, I'm sorry. Then he'd cut some more bread, very carefully, using the last slice as a thickness guide, and scrape the crumbs with the back edge of the knife into a perfect square on the breadboard. Then he'd cry again. Nobody took any real notice. There was a woman who spoke incessantly. Very conversational, confiding. She'd put her hand on Leverton's arm, told him something he couldn't begin to understand, about people he'd never heard of. Leverton had to put out the plates, the glasses, the knives and forks. Twenty places. Everybody had their own little task. Bryce Fuller showed him where everything was, which plates to put out. He'd tried. Moved about, smiled abstractedly, made way for people carrying great bowls of fruit, a platter of cold cuts. The knives did it. He scooped up a fistful from the drawer, got such a jangle, such a vitriolic hiss of spite, that he threw them on the floor, holding his hand like he'd been burned. He couldn't tell exactly what they were saying, but the tone was so sharp he didn't want to hear it. Fuller was right by his side, bending to pick them up.

—It's okay, Ken, he said. It's okay. I'll drop these right in the machine there. We have a bunch of knives.

By the time Fuller had loaded the knives into the dishwasher, Leverton was gone. He was outside, breathing in the scents of the evening shadows, eyes closed. His left knee was shaking, so he leaned over, put his hand on it, locked it back, staring at the grass.

—What are you thinking about? Fuller said.

Leverton filled his lungs, breathed out slowly. I heard stuff in there, he said. Not good. Sharp, cutting, not good.

—Was it what people were saying? Was it Susie? She says a lot of stuff. It's not your journey.

Leverton stood up and smiled at him. No, he said, it wasn't Susie. She the one that talks all the time? I couldn't understand a word she was saying. Anyway, that wasn't really what I was thinking about. I stopped listening to that stuff. When the voices aren't there they don't trouble me.

—So what were you thinking about? Exactly when I asked you?

Leverton looked at Fuller, this gentle guy, asking the right questions.

—Kirby Klein, he said. Kirby Klein.

Fuller pulled at the lobe of his ear. I'll bring some food out, we'll sit under the tree over there, okay? I'll be right back.

Leverton wandered over to the bench. He didn't want to hear it, dull stuff, railing talk, fencing, furniture, that insistent dumb complaint, banal observation. He sat on the grass nearby, watched Fuller come out of the kitchen with a tray of food. Fuller sat down cross-legged next to him, put the tray between them. Salad, cheese, some cold meat, couple of apples. Fruit juice. Bread.

—Eat, Ken. This is not a suggestion. Pick something up and put it in your mouth. Like this, see? Then, you chew . . .

Fuller took a bite from an apple, talked through it. Why were you thinking about Kirby?

Leverton weighed a slice of bread in the palm of his hand. I just think I missed her, that's all. I think there was a chance back there and I just blew it. Maybe more than one chance. I thought I was doing the right thing, by holding back? Thought I was being considerate. And it's too late. I fucked up with my wife. Then I fuck around for twenty years. I stop myself from falling in love without even realizing that's what I'm doing. I control everything, keep everything calm

121

and quiet. And now it's too late. I'm too old and too crazy and suddenly I miss that girl so much it hurts. So I guess I feel sick. I ache. That answer your question?

—Does it for you?

— It's as close as I can get. What's the point? I'm not here because of her. I'm here because I'm hearing voices again.

—But you're not hearing them now? Eat. Eat. Talk and eat.

—I hear stuff that has been made. Stuff that's been formed or assembled, not natural stuff. Not rocks and grass or plants. That would be almost okay, wouldn't it? Mystical. A gift or something, like I was in tune with the natural world. A blessing. I get crap from vending machines. I hear parking meters counting, I hear telephones going hysterical. All the most trivial shit. Best stuff was from my guitar, but I had to set it free, let it loose in the wild again to be with its guitar buddies, get some electricity through it. And I got patronized by my car. I'm cursed, Bryce. This is a fucking curse.

—This why you're not sitting on the bench?

Leverton nodded, chewing the bread without pleasure or hunger. Touching stuff helps, he said, if that's the right word. Most of the time. Makes the connection clearer. Although I do focus in on other stuff without touching it, depending upon how insistent it is, how receptive I am, I don't know.

—You want to tell me what the bench says?

—No. You wouldn't want to hear. It's really boring. You have no idea. It'd probably complain about the weight of the asses it has to put up with, if a slat needs repairing, whatever. And the effort would give me a headache.

—And you talk back? Every time?

—Not every time. Not much I can think of saying to a bunch of knives.

—And it's understandable. Both ways. You speak the same language.

—Yeah, you could say that. I assumed we talk English, but I'm not so sure. It's like there's this translation going on? Leverton wobbled an apple on the tray with a forefinger. You don't believe any of this, do you?

—Well, it's happening for you, Ken. I don't have restrictions on reality, normality, what is believable. There is no house style for truth here. You know that. We have people here who believe they're worthless, believe all kinds of things. It's not my job to share beliefs. Pete Ross tells me you check out okay on the simple stuff. Heartrate, blood pressure, reflexes, weight. You're in good shape.

Leverton couldn't help but smile at this. Oh, sure, he said. Never better. So, I'm going to sleep under the stars tonight, right?

—Matt's fixing you a sleeping-bag. Could start a trend. Been a long time since I lay and stared up at the night sky. Want some company?

—I'm not a good talker right now. Thanks.

—Matt'll be on hand. We'll give you his beeper.

—Uh, no thanks. I want to be alone. Circuitry, chips, you wouldn't believe. Know what they call us? The half-world, dumb muds.

Fuller raised his eyebrows, his forehead furrowed like sand combed by a child's beach rake. Dumb muds?

—And believe me, that's what you feel like, listening in. There's this whole other thing going on out there. Whole other thing.

Leverton bit into an apple, shifted position to ease the pressure on his knees. Fuller turned his head to look back across the grass at the house, windows glowing like a child's

123

Christmas card under the darkening sky. He knew Leverton just needed time to himself right now.

—You going to be okay for a while? he said. I should really get back. Matt will be right out with your stuff. You need me, anytime, press the buzzer by the lightswitch in there. Any lightswitch. Red buzzer. We'll know where you are.

—The panic button. Right.

Fuller reached across and rested a hand on Leverton's shoulder, pressing his fingers against the muscle strung across the blade. You're still pretty tense here, he said. We'll get you a massage in the morning. Bit of hands–on stuff. Has an effect. And just a quick note . . .

He moved his hand from Leverton's shoulder and touched the crease between his eyebrows with his index finger. This, he said. Try to smooth it out. Just as an exercise. See if you can figure out how. Change your face. No big deal. Don't sweat it, okay? I'll check back later. You want a book or something? Candle?

—Thanks, but I really appreciate the quiet. I'm okay, really.

Fuller nodded briefly and got to his feet like he'd floated up suddenly into his natural position. There was such a fluid efficiency in his every move it was a pleasure to watch. Leverton closed his eyes and breathed in the twilight. He needed the quiet, so he could see Kirby Klein. She came to him. The scent of her hair. Beach grass. He'd been close enough a couple of times. Close enough, but too far away. The tiny crescent creases that appeared at one corner of her mouth that said she believed nothing, but it amused her anyway. The way she wore sunglasses because her eyes gave

her away. How much did she know him? He pinched his
finger and thumb together. Half this, he whispered. Nothing.
All this noise, all the chaos, when it cleared away, when his
head was empty, he saw Kirby Klein, on a wave of longing
and loss that swept him out somewhere into the cold depths.

When Dean Mance got home he made a couple of calls,
took a shower, and made another call standing naked in front
of the mirror in the hallway, sucking up his belly to define
his abs.

—I can't apologize enough for this afternoon, he said. My
mother was hospitalized, and I had to be there. Thank you,
no, I'm afraid she is not good. She has this infection or
something, I can't believe. She's kind of on life support right
now. Yeah. No problem. Sure, sushi sounds good. He
profiled his ass cheek, pinching in the big muscle at the top
of his thigh. He thumbed the end-call button.

—Kirby, he said. I'm eating out, okay? In the bedroom he
teamed a Versace rollcollar jacket with stone silk pants and a
black turtleneck, laying them out on the bed. Then he folded
the turtleneck away and took a new parchment-colored
Ralph Lauren tee from a stack in his closet. Tees don't wash
well, no matter what the quality. You could really only wear
them a couple times. Kirby? he said, and again, a little louder.
The pants looked wrong now. The jacket was right. Start
from there, build it together. Sushi. We're talking studied
informality here. Less is more. He saw his wife's closet was
open. It was empty. And the first thing he could think of
was, Fuck, we've been burgled. Some asshole stole my wife's
clothes. He went into his office, checked his Apple Macintosh was still there, his Bang & Olufsen. The fuck was going

on? He stood looking blankly around him, weighing the mobile in his hand, passing the ball of his thumb over the rubber buttons. No way he could understand this woman. He went back to the bedroom. Docker pants. The new pair. Button-fly. Perfect.

Nothing But Shadows

The stars were still there. Leverton lay on his back, hands behind his head, and considered why they reminded him of childhood but meant nothing in themselves. Stars were for children, or lovers maybe. They weren't up there for him, that was for sure. Nothing to do with him anymore. He was no longer enraptured by them, caught up in them, no longer owned them the way he had as a child, in the way he'd been swept away by the sight of the ocean. Different stars, different ocean. These were representations, reminders, merely marks. You used to know us, they said. Remember us? Remember the beauty? Before you knew we were beautiful? Now they were a pattern he couldn't join up except in a reductive way, a way that imposed order and organization and recognition. He knew they had been his, he knew they were lost. He used to fly up there, as a kid, his whole little heart going out to them. Now they were just lights in the sky. And the ocean was just water. He didn't need the stars or the ocean anymore and they'd died for him, unloved.

But at least it was quiet out here, and his head was his own again. He became aware of the crease between his eyebrows, that vicious pinched indent, and touched it with his fingertip, as Fuller had done. Don't sweat it, he'd said. Concentrating on flattening it out just deepened the incision.

He stretched it by running his fingers along his eyebrows. It had an effect, somehow. Made him feel more open, maybe.

He pulled the zipper of the sleeping-bag up to his neck and closed his eyes, and Kirby Klein came to him. He remembered the times when he could have leaned into her, to hold her to him, and hadn't. She was married. He was old. They were professional partners. There was no good reason why he should have held her, even once, and every good reason why he should not. If he died in the night, he told himself, at least I can say I restrained myself from reaching out to Kirby and fucking things up. That must count for something, right? I behaved myself. Impeccably. No way she wouldn't have been surprised, upset maybe. No good would have come of it. The number of times I held back, I deserve a medal. That time she stumbled against the edge of the pool in my office. Or when she got out the car that time, or at Le Park. Bunch of times. I could have fouled up badly. She needs support, not another old fool pawing at her. A friend, not another fallen lover writhing and sobbing at her tiny feet. She had that quality, guys just fell over for her all the time. Hard. She'd told him, because he was a friend, about these guys. One went to Bali, lived in a hut. Another wrote to her every day for a year, a real letter in the mail, asking her to marry him. She told him about these men not as a boast, but because she saw something wrong in her, something that got these guys to fall in love with her on a level she didn't understand and couldn't control. It didn't make her happy. She thought she screwed up people's lives. Two guys had left their wives for her, unasked, and she felt responsible for busting up marriages. So why Dean? he'd asked. No real answer. Physical attraction, and it had been fun, a lot of fun, at first. He fit the parameters, all her friends said so. They looked right together. Hey ho, you know?

Leverton thought about how she'd supported him in the last few days, how he'd used her, complicated her life. And he thought about the look in her eyes as she'd said goodbye. No way had that been love, now he thought of it. Pity, sure. Exhaustion, maybe. Had there even been love in Tara's eyes? Or any of the others? How was he to tell? What did he know about love?

He woke with voices in his head, and his face full of grass.

—*everything's breaking in the entropy rush*

—*spreading pool of silence*

He rolled over, looked for his watch, instant reaction, not there.

—*sickness*

—*not possible to measure*

Leverton sat up, looked about him, tried to get his bearings.

—*5671764147250734548534563456475344473073563 – 6565435624-632*

Couldn't see the house, just a low black line of shrubs at the top of the rise, trees behind him. He'd turned over in his sleep, rolled.

—*signals cease no warning*

—*carriers dying*

He placed his hands on the ground. Here. He moved his hands like metal detectors, brushing the grass, hearing the rush of words get louder or softer. A line under the ground, going up the slope to the house. No direction, no motion, this stuff wasn't traveling, it was just there, in the center of his head.

—Who are you? he said, his face close to the ground. He said it again, this time silently. Who are you? The voices fused with each other, formed impenetrable word clusters, and all the time the counting, counting. He didn't get an answer. This was a massive concentration of voices, swelling, peaking, retreating, all within the white static hiss he knew to be the primordial language, the raw material of communication. He kicked himself free of the sleeping-bag. There was no room for thought. No break, no space not filled with talk. He put the heels of his hands to his forehead, stretched his mouth in a wordless howl.

Matt heard the cry from his room. He was a light sleeper, used to being called by the panic button or a hand on his shoulder. He woke thinking it was an animal in the woods, but there was something human in it. Ken, he thought. He leaped from his bed, grabbing a flashlight, and ran barefoot into the park. It was silent now. He went to where he'd left Leverton barely two hours before. The bottle of water was there, tipped over, and the folded blanket in the plastic bag.

—Ken! he shouted. Nothing. He swung the flashlight beam around, called his name again. Matt saw his own shadow slant across the grass as a light went on back up at the house. He jogged down the incline to the woods, and saw the pod of the sleeping-bag like a chili pepper in the purple-gray grass. He ran to it, calling Ken's name, kicked it over, looking for what? He held his breath and listened to the dark, searching the edge of the woods with the flashlight, watching the shadows lurch over the trunks. Fuller was at his side now, pushing his head through a hooded sweat top.

—We lose him?

—He may be back up at the house. I don't know. I should have stayed closer to him.

130

Fuller shook his head, picked up the sleeping-bag. Uh huh, he said. Ken didn't want it. Not how we work here, you know that. Anyone can walk into the woods anytime. It's if they want to come back that matters.

—I hope he's okay. You heard that howl?

—Yeah, I heard it. No, he's not okay. Weird thing. Unreachable. You sense that?

—Yeah. Like you say, he has to want to be reached. I'll check out the woods for a while, okay? I'll beep you if I find him.

Fuller rolled up the sleeping-bag under his arm, said, I'll check back at the house. Maybe he heard something, freaked him out.

Matt went into the woods that separated the park from Mulholland Drive. He could hear cars in the distance. Twice he stopped when he heard something move in the darkness, called Ken's name. Fuller, back at the house, checked with the night staff, jogged to Leverton's cabin. The suitcase still stood at the end of the bed. Oh, Ken, he said. Where the heck are you, buddy? He took his portable from his pocket and dialed the police. Standard procedure. This happened from time to time. If Leverton was picked up on the street, they'd know who he was. Fuller patted the suitcase like it was a dog waiting for the return of its master.

Klein called the hospital from the car. Bobbie was stable. More than that, impossible to say. It was botulism, as far as they could tell. There were needle punctures under her eyes, in her eyebrows. Klein had driven to the club, gone through Bobbie's bathroom cabinet, found vials of Botox all over, new packs of disposable needles. She'd put them in a bag and cabbed them to the hospital, along with all the other medication in the cabinet, TriPansodol, a bunch of stuff. And then she'd gone home and packed most of her clothes into two suitcases and driven down the coast to Palos Verdes, trying to get her thoughts in order. At least Bobbie hadn't died yet, at least that. Everything was such a mess. She needed some time to herself. Tomorrow was Sunday, she'd maybe go to the beach, see a movie with a girlfriend. Think about how she was going to play it on Monday with Maitland. Couple of things she needed to ask him, but she knew he never responded to direct questioning about anything. Wasn't interested in the content of the answers, but the context of the questions. He said.

She took a left up Mosely Street and parked in Leverton's driveway. She'd call the cops about his car. Tomorrow. The house was intimidatingly empty. She changed the sheets in the bedroom, put her toiletries out on the shelf in the bathroom and her makeup on the bedroom cabinet. She looked for a radio, a TV, anything to break the silence, hummed to herself until it sounded scary. She hung some of her clothes in the closet next to Leverton's four suits. She unwrapped his pencil award from a rolled teeshirt and, after trying a number of places and thinking it looked out of place everywhere, put it on the mantelpiece in the living room next to the Zippo lighter. She'd call The Garden in the morning, check he was okay. This house. How could he live here for so many years in the quiet like this? She passed the blanked-off door to the other bedroom. Tomorrow, she thought. She washed, made up her couch bed. And she made the last call of the day.

In a crumbling stucco bungalow, discolored like a hundred-year-old wedding cake, Irving Mance slept on a narrow sheetless bed, naked except for a fraying flesh-colored neck-brace, buckles encrusted with bright orange rust. In the dusty flicker of light from the chattering Super8 projector, his hair looked like wet paint on his forehead, and his plump, hairless breast shivered with an irregular heartbeat. In the center of the room a mothwinged screen caught the mute image of Bobbie Herrera in *The Gladiator's Challenge*. The telephone rang from the cluttered table at the end of the couch, making the pill bottles cluck and stutter. In his dream, perhaps, he took the call on-set, and barked orders through a white megaphone. A snore snapped in his throat, and he flinched from his sleep with his one good eye blinking in gummy film. He sat up, head swimming in a shower of sliding stars, fumbled the telephone to his ear. On the screen Bobbie Herrera, in her one starring role, made goo-goo eyes at Steve Reeves in bleached Todd-AO color. Yeah, he said. What? You woke me.

—It's Kirby.

—I recognized your voice, he said slowly, remembering the name from somewhere. He patted his hair back into a thin black stripe from ear to ear. What can I do for you?

—You should know about Bobbie.

I know about Bobbie, he said, watching her twist her hair in her fingertips and pout, those fabulous tits in profile from any angle. What about her? he said.

—She's really sick, up at the hospital. Really sick.

There was another pause, longer. Steve Reeves jumped onto a white horse. Bobbie Herrera waved from an archway. How's my son? he said. The good son. That never calls his father. How's Dean?

—He's the same. I guess. You want her room number?

Irving Mance repeated Bobbie's room number, got it

wrong. Klein patiently made him repeat it until he knew it. It's been a long time, he said. She won't want to see me.

—Sure she will. But she's sick, Irv. She may not be able to recognize you. I'm just telling you, okay? You can call the hospital. Tomorrow. You shouldn't make the trip yet. Listen, I have a question.

—I don't have any answers.

—You may to this. Bradley Brewster? Why does Bobbie have a photograph of him in her office?

She could hear his breathing, like somebody sawing through stale bread, and the morse code of a bottle neck on the rim of a glass.

—Irv? You okay?

—Bobbie, he said. I know it was my fault, but she wasn't right all the time, you know, some things, she had her reasons, I guess. Bradley. Jesus. Poor son of a bitch. Son of a bitch. My pills . . .

Klein heard muffled grunting, something knocked over, then his wheezing so close she pulled the phone from her ear. So, she said, why the photograph? What was he to Bobbie?

She heard his breathing turn into sobs. Her son, he said thickly. Told him before he got killed, but too late. Never forgave . . .

Klein strained to hear this. Had he said 'our son' or 'her son'? You're not his father? she said. Who's the father, Irv? She heard something fall, and maybe birdsong. Then quiet. She spoke his name several times. Goodnight, Irv, she said softly. You take care.

Irving Mance fell back onto the mattress, the tin bed zithering under his weight, and slipped his hand down over the milky pallor of his belly to pull at his prick, a soft purple

134

root in a damp steelwool nest. Bobbie leaned forward as she poured the wine into a jeweled goblet, her cleavage a chasm between clouds. Don't die, he said, a bead of phlegm chirring in his throat. Oh, don't die. Don't die.

Klein lay in bed for a while thinking. Thinking about Bobbie Herrera and her poor bastard son, and her drunken, impotent ex watching his old movies out at Zuma Beach. Watching them over and over. *Gladiator* movies. An Irving L. Mance Production. And Bobbie with tubes up her nose, lungs like wet paperbags, dreaming of days by the pool running with the Rat Pack, when she was young and golden and wanted.

And Dean. Dean she could cope with. She'd suddenly woken up to the fact that she just didn't like him. Hadn't liked him for some time. Worse; couldn't imagine why she'd ever liked him. If she ever had. Was it her? Whatever. He didn't talk to his mom, his dad, his wife. She wondered if he'd noticed she'd gone. He'd know when he played his messages. Hello, she'd said, I'm not here right now. If you'd care to leave a message, talk after the beep. Too subtle for him maybe. Dean Mance seemed like a very long time ago. Even his name seemed suddenly stupid. She'd asked Bobbie once, when they were looking at a picture of her with Dean Martin, what was going on here exactly. Why wasn't her son called Irving? Bobbie had looked at her totally blankly, said, Well, you wanted a husband called Irving? The photograph was signed 'To Bobbie, love you, love you. Dino'.

And now the guy in the background of another photograph, Bradley Brewster, still out of focus. Still there. In a lot of people's lives. Well, Klein said, there you go, gal, a bed to yourself in a crazy guy's house. And it could be so much worse. Life is sweet and good and full of surprises. She began

135

to cry again, just for a second, just until, sickened, she caught herself in the act of congratulating her own sensitivity.

Sleep was not an option. What was she doing here? She needed the company of a girlfriend, not this thick silence. She needed human conversation, not the sound of her own breathing. She swung her legs out of bed, went into the hallway. Here she was again. This empty theater, lit by leftover light from the street. She'd stared at this scenery before, wondered what lay behind. She leaned a hip against the blanked-off door. Nothing moved. She pushed the flat of her hand further up, away from where the handle would have been, felt the panel give a little, just a little. She kicked at it, heard the door snap back against the frame. Okay, she said. Time to open the box. She got dressed, went through into the garage from the hallway door. Everything neatly stacked, mountainbike hung on the wall, toolrack, everything new. She chose a heavy clawhammer, swinging it in her fist, went back into the house.

It didn't happen like she'd expected. The hammer went through the door panel, splintered back a circle the size of the hammerhead. Shit, she said. She swung it again, made the hole bigger. The door stayed shut. Well, she thought, no going back now, not going to get away with that. She smashed at the door, making the mess bigger, until she hit the lock, and knew where to aim. It hurt her wrist, the impact, and the sound was shocking, made her stop several times just to listen for the inevitable knock on the front door, the police flashlight through the window. Nothing. She gripped the hammer with both hands, swung again, awkwardly, mashing the frame, and the door opened. She dropped the hammer.

What does twenty years of dead air smell like? Like death

must smell. She nudged the door wide with her toe, hand over her mouth and nose. This is terrible, she thought. I'm doing something terrible. This is not my problem. Walk away. The room was dim, shadowed, sepulchral. She could see the foot of a bed, an open chest of drawers, curtains at the window. And garlands of cobwebs, swinging in the first movement of air for two decades. Hanging across the yellowing folds of curtain, clinging like vines to the gray walls, drifting across the ceiling, cobwebs had made the room their own. The smell of dust and dead air was like grit in her throat, sweet-sharp, sickly. As her eyes got used to the light she saw a glittering black line on the carpet beneath the window, like an evening scarf or a thick diamante necklace. She fumbled inside the door, turned on the ceiling lamp. The room was clotted with a fluttering bruise of thick yellow light, the cobwebbed bulb burning dust. Before anything else, she saw that the black line under the window was a long heap of dead flies; inexplicable, horrible. She retched, swallowed it back. She turned her head away, looked around the room. Dressing table, drawers pulled open, tilted mirror, mottled like a turtle's back. Bare ring tree, empty jewelry case, the type you closed with ribbons. Open closet, bare except for one wire hanger. The bed a mess, sheets torn, in rags, spread over the floor. Clothes spilled from the chest of drawers.

There was a sheet of paper on the bedside table, and she picked it up, spilling something bright onto the floor. It rolled under the bed. She looked at the paper in her hand, a letter, big angry writing.

It's over. I can't take any more. Don't come after me. Goodbye. Sonia.

Something shiny had disappeared under the bed, but she knew what it was. A wedding ring. She knelt down, moved her hand over the carpet. It felt like stiff animal pelt, and in the faltering bloom of yellow light from the dying bulb she saw her hand livid against a shadow or a stain and a cobweb caressed her cheek, kissed her lip in the sudden dark.

She spent a couple of hours in the bathroom, dry-heaving into the toilet, taking a bath and a shower. Then she went into the kitchen, passing the door she'd pulled closed without a glance, tried to put together something to eat from the desiccated fronds of salad and herbs in the refrigerator. *It's over. I can't take any more.* She sat in the living room with all the lights on, legs drawn up underneath her on the couch. *Don't come after me. Goodbye.* She shuddered. She'd taken the letter with her when she ran from the room. It was on the cushion next to her. Folded twice, like it had been in an envelope. Only it hadn't. She put down the plate of picked-at food and folded the letter closed. The top fold was short, maybe by an inch.

Sonia. The woman who was in Canada. TV production work. Could that be checked? Maybe using a different name, her maiden name. Called Maitland from time to time. Sonia. So-near. Klein unfolded the letter, looked at the crazed, vicious pencil scrawl, so hard it tore right through the paper in three places. There was no name at the top, on the short fold. This was a short piece of paper, too. *Proportions aren't right. Nothing about this is right.* Okay, she thought, trying to order events in her mind. Twenty years ago, Leverton, ill with drink, discovered the room pretty much as she'd found it. He reads the note, goes on a three-year weekend. Just leaves the room and seals it up. *Don't come after me.* He hadn't

138

gone after her. The letter didn't have his name at the top. It had been on the bedside table, with the ring. Folded to fit a non-existent envelope. This didn't make sense. Make it make sense. Somebody has to. But if the letter had been sent to somebody else, through the mail, that would account for the folds. They'd cut their name off, put the letter in Sonia's room. With the ring.

This letter had never been meant for Ken, she thought. Sonia was finishing something with somebody else. That somebody had put the letter in her room, for Leverton to see. So Sonia being in Canada made no sense either, because if she'd finished with this somebody else, she could stay with Leverton. Also, think about it, she said to herself. Would you take all your jewelry from your jewel case if you were leaving in a hurry, or would you just take the case? She knew the answer to this one. Her jewelry box was in her suitcase. She'd snapped the lid shut, packed it away. Five seconds. Maitland was getting calls from Sonia. Nothing made any sense. It was late, and she was too tired to think. She curled up on the couch and was asleep before her plate slid to the floor, unheard. The fork rang on its tines, was silent.

Around the small sea-shell curve of her exhausted body the gray room glimmered, airless, soundless. And when first light crept across the walls it revealed nothing but shadows.

All He Was

At some point it had become obvious that he had to get to Klein, that there was no choice, that there was nobody else, and nothing else mattered. Didn't want to talk to anybody else, look at anybody else. Didn't want Bryce Fuller's quiet counsel, didn't need the hippie community vibe of The Garden. Didn't want to join in. Didn't want help or understanding. He knew that he had to be with her, that everything else was a waste of time. A fake. How long had he known this? It seemed like it had just happened that moment, a hundred years ago. He tried to remember the look she'd given him as she said goodbye. Did she just care for him, feel sorry for him? Or want him? This sick old guy with the voices in his head? He didn't know, didn't care. Yes, he cared. It was the only thing that mattered.

He could feel the wires in him, pulling him to her. His body was wired into her, his stomach ached, his whole body ached with her name. He couldn't keep still. Fuck the stupid voices. Fuck the sickness. If she didn't love him, it was nothing but noise. Nothing but noise anyway, the empty boneyard rattle chatter and idiot clatter of communication. Here in the woods he could hear his heart, and he knew it was Kirby Klein's. Knew now, when he was lost above Topanga Canyon somewhere, skirting people's homes like a mad dog, scratching between nameless shrubbery, twisting his ankle on unseen rubble. He knew too late. Too late to hold her to him in the shining mundanity of the parking lot, the restaurant, the deserted office. The moments he'd held back, the moments gone forever. You fuck. He began to cry. Stopped. Started again. You stupid old fuck. You deserve what you get. Shut everybody out for so long you get voices in the head. You're on your own, you're old and you're wrecked and you're on your own.

He struggled up over a dark rise, a high concrete wall with a frosting of broken glass to his left, the blank back wall of somewhere to his right. LA flared suddenly before him, brighter than an ocean, and a tidal wave of deafening white noise rose up the mountainside and flooded over him. He stood and swayed in terrible rapture, the air like static in his pumping lungs. His eyes were filled with the surge of the city, the silicon sliver of sparks that hid the deep subterranean shapes, and he heard the rolling beasts beneath that would someday rise and break the surface, as everything hidden must. He swooned, skidded on a crushed drinks can, grabbed a sharp branch. Out of breath, out of shape, out of luck, out of time. Kirby, he said aloud. Kirby! He slumped, fell. Helicopters? He crawled over some kind of concrete ledge, foundation or ruin. Voices crackled about him, within him, ran through him like fire, like gunfire. He remembered now, in the confusion, the jungle, and that crawling feeling of being alone and watched. Where were they? Sodium shadow. Faces glimpsed in flaring smoke. Shining with sweat. Kirby! Hear me. Kirby. Hear me. Hear my voice in your head. Kirby! Kirby! Kirby! A broken wall. Maintain position. The muffled pillow thump of mortar. Firecracker smell. Beautiful. Thin ribboning stutter of M16s. Cellophane crackle of small-arms fire. And the voices; those shrieks torn from throats too small to birth them, ripped right out of the hearts of the poor fuckers burned and bleeding and beyond help. In the jungle, Leverton crawled to the wall. Crawl to the wall. Bleeding fingers. Pull up, over, stay low. Stay low! You fuck! You fuck! Shadows fractal-edged in razor clarity. Kirby! Where were they? Back in the jungle and smoke. This was fucked.

—*Kirby!*

He staggered to his feet and tried to cry her name, the only thing he knew. Blown apart and filled with noise, with voices from nowhere, from everywhere, a hook remained in his heart. He howled her name, yet couldn't hear it, deaf or dumb or dead. He howled her name, yelled it and spelled it in his head and his heart. It was inside him, attempting to rise, a massive mute embolism, anchored at great depth, a dark bubble that never broke free. Suffocated, drowned, the word swelled; a still-born iteration that engorged his throat and mouth in phantom nativity, then aborted in a numb spread of soundless pain. Fists in his eyes, he fell in the dark, lungs bursting in the undertow of something that had passed, something he knew he had missed forever, something that left him nothing but void, a ruin, a vast sunless space that reverberated with the echo of her name.

—*Kirby.*

He knew her name. It was all he had. All he was.

Paradise Fucked

—What do you mean, you lost him?

—Mrs Klein—

—You lost him? How can you just lose somebody? How?

—We have informed the police. There's a standard procedure . . .

—A standard procedure? Wait. I don't get this.

—We are not a secure institution. This is always made clear. If somebody wants to walk out, they can walk out. It does happen. Not often, but it does happen. They walk in, they walk out. There's no coercion either way.

—So when did you lose him? Exactly?

—Matt heard him at around three a.m. We searched the grounds for an hour. Called the police.

—Heard him what?

—It's not clear. Some kind of cry. He was sleeping outside, as he needed the quiet. Matt's not sure what he heard. Ken wouldn't take a beeper, said it would be too noisy. We found his sleeping-bag, and think he walked into the woods.

—Why? Why would he walk into the woods?

—Mrs Klein, please, we have no idea. Ken is pretty strung out. He may be beyond our help this time. I remember him from way back, the first time. He was a long way out then, but he wanted to be reached. This time, I don't know. We did all we could, and like I say, the cops are out there. He may even just walk back. Or call you. He talked about you a lot.

—He did? What did he say?

—We never give out that kind of detail. I will say you mean a lot to him, that's evident. That's why I called you first thing. He may be on his way to you. And if you see him, you must call me here. Don't worry about the police, I'll handle that end. Just let me know directly you hear from him, okay? In the meantime, he's being looked for. He'll turn up. We'll find him.

—And you call me if you do, okay? I'm going to worry myself sick about this.

—I'll call personally. That's a given. I'm sorry it's happened this way, really. Try not to worry. That's facile, I know, but it's also good advice.

—Okay. Let's be in touch, okay?

Klein folded her mobile shut. She was stiff from sleeping on the couch. She worked the hinges of her jaw with her fingertips, stretched. What time was it? What day was it? Her mouth felt clammy. She tried to remember her yogic salute to the sun. Beautifully balletic set of movements. Got it in the wrong order, somehow, got it wrong. She didn't even look at the broken door as she passed it. She showered, dressed, drank a glass of milk, and drove the Porsche up the San Diego freeway to the office at Century City. Forgetting how to do her salute to the sun, that bothered her. Like forgetting your name.

Maitland's car was in his slot under the SS&T building. She knew he'd be here, putting in a couple hours' work, preparing for Monday's meetings. He always did. She rode the elevator to the MLA floor and used her swipecard on the lock. The empty suite seemed at once lifelessly hollow yet shrill with expectancy; a surprise party for a ghost. Klein stood and listened to the electrically charged silence, looked around, eye caught by the profile of someone at Austin's desk. It was the big cutout of Jerry Seinfeld holding a muffler, propped up in his chair. She walked down the corridor, past her own office, and tried Leverton's door, just for the heck of it. It swung open. She saw the drooping white flowers on Fee's desk, the blinds lowered against the glare, the square pool, still as a slab. She went to his desk, sat in his chair. It seemed like a lifetime ago, ducking in to remind him of the TasteLicious presentation. And his disturbing crazy-guy laugh in the middle of her pitch, when everyone had looked at him over their shoulder. That had been the first sign that something had gone badly wrong inside him.

She thought back to the first time they'd met, at Le Park. She'd been invited to a product launch and Maitland made the introduction, saying Leverton was his oldest friend and the only guy he could trust in this town. This was what everybody said about everybody else in LA, but there had been something in Leverton's look, a kind of awkward modesty perhaps, that made it look as if the words meant something. Leverton seemed to know, or imagine, that he wasn't the sexy one of the partnership. He was older, lacked Maitland's hypnotic intensity, and there was an air of something held back about him that Klein warmed to immediately.

The first thing she'd said, or nearly the first, was that he reminded her of somebody. Leverton had grinned and said, Yeah, Fred Flintstone. I get a lot of that. Klein laughed, and yes, there was something about the blue chin and thick black hair. She found herself smiling at the memory, sitting in his chair. There'd been times when she'd found herself attracted to him, just moments, but nothing had ever happened. She knew he respected her as a professional partner, but that was as far as it went. She'd leaned into him once or twice, almost by accident, the way these things happen, but he hadn't responded. A guy who'd sobered up twenty years ago to find his heart broken, and lived in a kind of arm's-length isolation ever since. What had Bryce Fuller said? That he didn't want to be reached? That was so right.

She idly slid open his telephone drawer and a card flipped out, caught in a runner at the side of the tray. She bent to pick it up. Blue file card, blank both sides. How appropriate. She pinched it between finger and thumb. How much do I know about him? This much. Half this. Nothing.

Something made her glance up. Maitland stood in the door, looking like a catalog model in casual weekend clothes. His pose was perfect, forearm resting on the doorframe at head height, hand falling so you could see the Cartier Tank watch, his weight on one leg, right hand in the pocket of his pleated khakis.

—Kirby, he said.

—Hi.

He came into the room, sat on the low slate surround to the pool, hitching his pants legs at the knee. You were missed, he said.

—I'm sorry?

—At the party. I called for you to come up, take a bow for the TasteLicious account, you weren't there.

Klein paused for a while. She remembered her anger, and strengthened herself with it instead of letting it make her stupid.

146

—You know where I was, of course.

Maitland looked puzzled. I'm sorry?

—Check the film in your camera. Or am I already on the wall?

—What? His bafflement, so out of character, seemed utterly real. Klein felt the subtle landslip of doubt undermine her anger. The shape against the balcony window, the flash of something. Shanna saying, Welcome to the gallery. What had she seen? Anything?

—I was at Shanna's place, she said. I saw her gallery. All those shots taken from the house. Didn't know you were interested in photography.

Maitland's expression reverted to the emotionally inert gaze he used habitually. His face held the same kind of flat fascination as a Warhol multiple; you looked at it repeatedly, searching for differences, some clue to the feeling that hid beneath.

—Work bring you in today? he said.

—No, I wanted to talk. Ask you a couple questions.

Maitland made a small opening gesture with his hands. My time is yours, he said.

—First, I want to clear this Bradley Brewster thing up.

She left a pause. Maitland turned slightly toward her, rested his chin in his hand, wristwatch flashing in a band of light that cut between the window blinds, dividing the room like a thick pane of edge-lit green glass. In leaning forward his face had entered the band, and his eyes reflected a water-colored light that never flickered. He said nothing.

—You said just now that I was missed, she said. But I missed you more back then, when I was working to land the account. It wasn't so much your lack of support, which was obvious enough, as your actual disincentive, which I couldn't understand at the time. And I felt hurt by. But now I think I do understand. Your wife, ex-wife, whatever, had been involved with Bradley Brewster. Recently enough to make the connection a potential embarrassment. It was a connection you couldn't control. This guy was probably murdered. You didn't know if the cops would turn up, following a lead back to her house, maybe back to you. So you actually discouraged me from working on the account. And when I reeled it in, against all your expectations, you consciously backgrounded yourself. As I said to Ken, how like you is that? Centerstage is where you're at your best. More than that, centerstage is where you are, wherever you are. But not this time. Ken thought you were giving me my space, but now I know. And you're still concerned that this thing is going to come to the surface, of course. The cops could come to your house at any time.

Klein searched Maitland's face for some kind of indication she was on track. Nothing. He'd moved back out of the light, and his eyes were blank, unblinking, looking somewhere over her shoulder. Then she realized she was looking in the wrong place. The hand at his knee. The fingers had tightened almost imperceptibly, the nails angled in slightly, raising the cuff of his pants. It wasn't much, but it was enough. She saw the muscles in his throat twist like a rope as he swallowed before he spoke.

—I acted appropriately to the context.

So that was it, she thought. That was all she would get out of him.

—I'm still not complete on the Brewster thing, she said. She placed her fingertips on the edge of Leverton's desk, feeling the slide of her nails against the wood. There's a missing here, she said, using Maitland's own vocabulary. You

148

were also aware, and how I don't know, that Bobbie Herrera, my mother-in-law, was Brewster's mother. This was another connection. This is the reason you're moving the account to Peter. Another distancing exercise.

Maitland stood up, moved to Fee's desk and fingered the little white flowers. A few petals fell like paperweight snow.

—Kirby, he said. Whatever my reasons, the decisions I take are for the benefit of the associates and their employees. That's the context for action here. Bradley Brewster screwed up everybody he came into contact with. Yes, I want to distance myself from him. If TasteLicious finds out he was staying at Shanna's house up until a month before he was found dead in a toilet, it will screw up the account. If they find out that your mother-in-law is also the mother of their biggest corporate embarrassment then that too will screw up the account.

He swept the petals off the edge of the desk into the palm of his hand and looked at them. There is also an aspect here you haven't worked through, he said. Peter has the account. If the account falls over, so does he. Not you, not me. And Peter is unaware of these connections, and he need never know. He must never know. And while I applaud your thinking here, and the logic and intelligence that inform it, it was not necessary for you to know, either. It must go no further.

He went to the pool and scattered the petals onto the surface, where they stuck, immobile, like it was a pool of tar. He brushed his hands together. Brewster was a fuck-up, he said. In a way it's better for everybody that he's not around anymore. Let him lie. Come into work tomorrow and be glad I've given Peter the day-to-day on TasteLicious. Forget it. Move forward. Tomorrow we'll talk strategy.

Klein thought, Forget it. Forget a violent death associated with the CEO of my firm.

—Thank you, she said. I'm complete on the Brewster thing.

Something close to a smile moved the corners of Maitland's mouth. Was there something else? he said.

—Yeah. If you have the time. Something worrying me.

—Like I say. My time is yours.

—Sonia Leverton.

This time she had him. His face twitched, and a hand went to his cheek to hold it.

—Sonia? What about her?

—Exactly.

He grinned, mere muscle movement around his mouth that left his eyes unaffected. Catalog grin. You're way off, Kirby, he said. Your powers of logical deduction have deserted you. And I can't imagine why you ask. I really can't. What made you think of her?

Klein clawed her nails up over the surface of the desk. Oh, she said, just trying to get the big picture here. Because something happened in the past doesn't mean it didn't happen. Like you say, these things have a way of coming to the surface. Just floating on up, when you least expect them.

—I said that? I don't think so. In any event, you're out of the loop here, Kirby. But I'm interested: what made you say that? What did you think the possibilities were? That I'd be offended? Or impressed? Or threatened? What conversation are you having here?

—How often do you hear from her?

—You have a way of answering questions with a question. It's not an invalid tactic, but it's tiring. To answer your question, not for some time. But we're having separate conversations here. Listen, we'll talk in my office at nine tomorrow morning, okay? But not about this, okay?

He walked to the door. She saw the self-consciousness in every step, like he was acting the walk. This was how you walked when you were unconcerned. You don't know what to do with your hands. This was the first time she'd ever seen him move like this, without that superbly poised self-confidence and strength.

—It's just odd, she said, raising her voice just enough to make him stop in the doorway, that the complications in your life have a way of, uh, distancing themselves. Sonia Leverton. Bradley Brewster. Klein paused, a mere beat. And Ken, she said. She saw his big shoulders tighten under his shirt.

—Nine o'clock. My office.

She heard him walk down the corridor and push through the door, the soft click as it swung closed.

—Nine o'clock, my ass, she said.

Leverton woke with the familiar rush of voices in his head, so strong he had difficulty distinguishing the feeble thread of his own thoughts, the top-note of conversational conscious-ness that normally keeps us company. It seemed to him that the voices had been there in sleep, too, inseparable from dream. Just above his head leaves intertwined against a silver-blue sky; he lay in a kind of hammock of long stems and leaves, formed by his fall, one leg up on the low wall he remembered, dimly, crawling over. He tried to level out the sounds in his head, to flatten them into background. He had to move. He knew he was probably lying on a cable or telecommunications route. Only electronics made such an

insistent, overwhelming clangor. He unhooked the heel of
his shoe from the broken top of the wall, felt the numbness
in his foot spread up his leg like fire. He rolled onto his
hands and knees, feeling his sweatshirt snag against a barbed
stem, and seeing dried blood caked around his fingernails.
He spoke to himself.

—*Okay, Ken. Get up. Walk.*

His voice joined the others in his head, but didn't leave
his mouth. There was no vibration in the throat, just Novo-
cain. He tried again.

—*Hello. Hello.*

He was aware of his voice occupying its own frequency
amongst the others in his head. He found a rock under his
hand and scraped it along the wall, banged it against the soft
cement. Nothing. He knelt and clapped his hands together.
Nothing. No sound.

—*Oh fuck, oh shit, oh help me . . .*

And this time there was an answer.

—*and no help anywhere.*

Maybe just a random thread, snaking up to the surface, a
fragment like the others, rising and falling in its turn. Leverton tried to grab it.

—*Hello?*

Nothing. He shook his head, stood up, holding onto his
knees, pushing up through the plants knotted over his back.
A swell of voices made him tilt, sick with vertigo, and he
grabbed the top of the wall to steady himself.

—*Got to get away from here. Move your legs.*

He hauled himself up over the wall, rolled over the top.
Over to the left, across a broken concrete floor, a flight of
steps climbed up alongside a windowless wall trellised in
graffiti. He staggered toward it. That unbearable babble

diminished as he dragged his numb leg behind him, stamped it to shake the ants out of his foot.

—*Come on, come on.*

He climbed the stairs, the rusted iron plates flaking and shivering underfoot. He couldn't hear the fall of his foot on the metal, just the dull, grating, monosyllabic complaint about his weight on the bolts in the wall. Where was he? Leverton reached the roof with nowhere else to go.

—*Kirby.*

The voices in his head reduced to a dull idiot mumble. Leverton sat on the edge of the roof. In a city whose center is nowhere, where you are always on the edge by definition, whirling on the perimeter, this was truly the epicenter of nowhere at all. Broken brick, weed-strewn rubble, surrounded by the gentle woodland of the Santa Monica mountains, like a dried-up head wound surrounded by waves of beautiful hair. The city lost in morning haze far below, a translucent metalflake phosphorescence that passed itself off as beauty, a chemical glamor seductive as the alpine glint of pure heroin.

He felt a hand on his shoulder and whirled around, unbalanced.

—Hey, careful. Don't want to fall off.

Leverton saw the kid's mouth move, heard nothing. He was maybe eighteen, with corn-row hair bleached yellow and a row of rings piercing one eyebrow. He wore ripped jeans, laceless sneakers, and was barechested, with a dark geometrical tattoo over his heart.

—You okay? he said.

—*Can you hear me?*

He squatted next to Leverton and frowned at him. You got a voice? You dumb or something?

—I can't hear you.

The kid shook his head. No good, he said. We ain't getting nowhere. You want a drink? He mimed holding a can up to his mouth, swallowed, wiped his mouth with the back of his hand. Leverton nodded, and watched the kid spring to his feet and cross the roof to an open hatchway, dropping down into it to return a moment later with a half-empty plastic bottle of cola. The kid sat next to him, took a gulp and wiped the neck before passing it over.

—'S'warm, he said. Ain't got no 'frigerator. Ha ha! I got plenty, they don't function too good, is what I'm saying. Limited functionality.

As Leverton took the bottle his hands shook violently. The kid helped him close his fists around the sticky plastic.

—You in a bad way. You a wino?

Leverton tried to read the kid's lips, shook his head. He drank from the bottle, warm and sticky and flat, but it sluiced the bitter cement dust from his teeth. The kid pulled it away before he could drain it. C'mon, said the kid. Got something to show you. It's a secret, but as you deaf and dumb I figure you the ideal person to tell, okay?

Leverton stood up uncertainly, followed the kid to the circular hatchway, surrounded by a crumbling brick edge. The low sun didn't yet reach down into it, obsidian, depthless. The kid swung over the edge, dropped out of sight. Leverton sat on the ledge and dangled his feet into the black, straining to see. He felt hands guide his feet to rungs set into the wall, and turned around so he could slide down over the ledge on his belly. He let himself down into the darkness.

The kid led him by the sleeve along a black corridor into a large room like a factory floor, with small-paned grimy windows in the wall which faced the city, letting in a

154

scummy bathwater light. A massive round wooden table in the middle, split into two semicircles with rusty seats between them, like tractor seats set on poles in the floor. Broken machinery and trailing cables hung from the ceiling, and a circular track, now buckled and broken, hung above the table like a cemetery halo.

—Use to be the American Parachute Company, the kid said. Where they made the parachutes? For the war? Anyhow, it's my place now. I use to be living on the Strip, but my collection got too big. I was on *The Shuggy Show*? I took some of my shit on his show, let him treat me like a nut, I didn't care. Right now, after all the work I done, I'm relieved if people think I'm a nut. It was too early to tell people, see? Didn't have enough evidence.

Every available surface, including the floor, was piled with what looked like stuff picked up off the street; smashed televisions were stacked, ceiling high, in one corner, rusty refrigerators in another. The circular table displayed bits of electronics or machine innards, grouped together and labeled. A half-dozen or so mashed and wheelless supermarket carts were bunched together next to a sprawling heap of wire hangers. Car parts were arranged in as orderly heaps as their shapes allowed. Leverton could make out at least eight powerplants, and a row of rusty and twisted mufflers stacked against the wall near the door. Everything identified with paper labels. He lifted one in his fingers; indecipherable squiggles, not real writing. The kid was a nut.

—All this stuff, see, the kid said, gesturing around the room, is evidence. Evidence. And I'm the only living motherfucker who knows what's going on. Check this shit out, man, check it out, I tell you something.

Leverton was trying both to lipread the kid and to suppress

the rising murmur of voices in the room. He mimed writing on the palm of his hand, like he was asking for the check in a restaurant.

—You wanna write me something? Okay. I got stuff here.

The kid went to a dented filing cabinet and took a sheet of Chateau Marmont writing paper from a file, and a blunt pencil stub from his pocket. Here you go, he said. Leverton found a space on the circular table between a heap of old typewriters and a cardboard box of smashed plates and wrote:

My name is Ken Leverton. I have lost my voice and my hearing. I need to get in touch with someone called Kirby Klein. I need urgent help. Please call her on this number and tell her how to find me. Thank you.

He added her mobile telephone number and passed the sheet of paper to the kid, who glanced at it cursorily.

—What you may or may not have noticed, see, about all this shit is that it don't work. The functionality is, as I said, limited. To the point where it's all fucked. None of this shit works. Now what interests me, see, is this state of not-working-ness fucked-up-ness is generally misunderstood amongst the people. Come here, come on over here, man.

He walked toward the windows, beckoning Leverton with the letter. Leverton followed, the tapping metronomic voices from the typewriters getting a little less distinct as he moved away from them. He pointed at the sheet of paper in the kid's hand.

—*The letter. Read the letter.*

The kid smeared a circle in the dust on a windowpane and peered through it. He started speaking quietly, almost to himself.

156

—Out there, there is no comfort. No tenderness. Know this place? LA is the most comfortless place on the planet. You can buy anything you want. You can buy rich. You can buy pussy. Pussy any age, any kind. Hot or cold. You can buy any drug you want and a few they ain't thought of yet. You can buy diseases from other planets. You can buy salvation from any motherfucking religion you want and you can buy a date with some sick fuck who's been eating straw to make his shit solid enough to fuck you in the ass. You can get your fucking lawn psychoanalyzed and your face to look like a zoo animal. You can legally get married to your mother and you can get dead in more ways than the police know about, but you can't buy no comfort. There is no comfort out there, man. No tenderness.

He turned from the window, and there was a hardness in his face that wasn't there before, a tightening, as if he was trying not to cry. His voice rose steadily, and he gritted his teeth between sentences, clenching his jaw, tightening his fists so the muscles in his arms swelled and locked.

—Every one of us motherfuckers is on his own, and don't kid yourself. You come in alone, you go out alone. If you got some other motherfucker to hold your hand in the dark, that's as good as it gets and you can die a lucky man. There's no such thing as being together. There is no tenderness, no comfort. Everything is apart, we're all lonely and busted up, and that's the way it is.

He held up Leverton's letter to the weak light that filtered through the window. It was a string of marks like some alphabet thought up by a child; random, ugly, meaningless, trailing off like an unfinished thread. The kid looked at Leverton wandering amongst the junk and laughed briefly.

—Not only can't you speak or hear, man, you don' write

too good neither. You are somebody really special, you know that? Let me finish here. You know 'bout entropy? I did some research. It's the stuff that busts shit up, stops it working. All this busted shit that I have so laboriously collected and gathered together here in my domain is evidence of entropy. And I observe this shit, and I think about it, and a picture is emerging for me. You know those guys that look for lights in the sky? Or conspiracy nuts? Or Jesus freaks? Or whatever. They're all looking in the wrong place, man. The wrong place. The evidence is everywhere. In the street. In the little shit, the stuff that gets discarded and ignored and thrown away. It's all evidence. You can't ignore it. I tag it all, I have a police procedure here.

And I tell you what it's evidence for, what all this broken and non-functional stuff is telling me. That everything – every motherfucking thing – is falling apart. That there is no coming together. No big fucking universal hug, no communication whatsoever. There is trouble in paradise, the walls are down, and the palace of love is a ruin. And fucking, coming together, and we don't stay together, you will have noticed, you die a little in there, man, fucking is just a way to bring another separate thing into the world, another broken bit of apart-ness, that making love is the right phrase, because it don' exist unless you make it, and every motherfucking thing that's made gets broken, love too, every motherfucking thing put together falls apart and blows away on the wind and there ain't a fucking thing you can do about it. It's entropy in the heart. God don' work no more, God is fucked, and the Garden of Eden is full of busted shit. And that's the truth. It's God that holds together, and God is busted, and everything is falling apart. You can look in all my shit here, take a look, check it out. Not going to find

God anywhere, I absolutely guarantee it. And the big secret, the secret behind the secret, is that this shit is happening faster. I'm measuring it. I keep records. Entropy is speeding up, man.

He had spoken in a rush, a stuttering rap, like he'd run through this many times, and he'd spoken for his own benefit, not even noticing Leverton, who'd wandered off amongst the debris, bending to touch a bike frame twisted into a pretzel, or a shard of car tire, or sift through a box of dirty doll parts, listening to the rubble of talk in his head, the broken clumps of language, the torn, distended threads of memory that inhabited these poor, amputated things on the edge of the world, on the edge of existence, and hearing nothing but isolated regret, no communication, no sharing, no togetherness, and a pain so habitual, so much part of memory itself, as to be almost anesthetic.

The kid looked out of the window again, pressing his face up to the cracked glass, and he spoke in a breath. And you sure as hell ain't going to find God out there, in the city of the motherfucking angels.

Standing back from the window, he sucked a lungful of air into his skinny frame, drew back his fist and thrust it forward straight from the shoulder, punched out a single pane of glass, stood like that, immobile, carved in a moment, before pulling his fist back through the jagged hole in the same straight piston line. A star of sunlight from the broken pane emblazoned the tattoo on his breast like you could see his blue heart beating through the skin. He briefly examined his hand for cuts, Leverton's letter falling to the floor like a leaf, and his shoulders relaxed.

—Paradise lost, he said. Paradise fucked.

Nothing

There were flowers. Yellow roses. A gentle chorus, their scent and color softening and illuminating the space, to the extent of making the room, with its comfortless functionality, seem in some way an extension of the nature of the blooms; as if the bed, and the steel table, the ticking box from which snaked taped tubes of clear liquid, even Bobbie Herrera herself, were fragile projections of their cadmium light, no more substantial than the image on a cinema screen.

Herrera's closed eyes were visible above the plastic and gauze mask, her eyebrows shaved, the row of hypodermic punctures clearly visible, like the trail of a rusty sewing machine. Her hair was pushed back under a plastic showercap the same transparent turquoise as the tubes going into her mask. Klein watched her eyes flicker in dream. Was she golden and young again? Was she being carried by Peter Lawford, her head thrown back in a squeal of delight and provocative helplessness? Was she slipping between satin sheets with Dean Martin, imported champagne cooling in a frosted silver bucket by the bed? Where was she?

—Bobbie?

Could she hear anything? Anything like an echo from the room in which she lay, as her wild hot spirit danced in the violet lights of the cage at the Cheetah?

—Bobbie? It's Kirby. I brought you flowers.

She stopped talking. It was like speaking into an answering machine. She cleared her throat. I wish you could see them, she said. They're beautiful. Dean sends his love, and he'll be by later, as soon as he can. He sent you flowers too, and Irv. Irv's fine, and maybe he'll come by too, when you're stronger. He's doing fine. We had a good long talk on the phone. There's a lot he wants to tell you, about how he knows he made mistakes, and he's sorry. Anyway. The doctor tells me you're making good progress. He's cute! You should really try to get a look at him, just one eye, okay? That's enough for a wink. You can do it!

Klein looked away. Looked at the single bunch of flowers she'd brought. She shut her eyes hard for a moment, took a couple of deep breaths. She was somehow aware of someone standing in the doorway and turned her head, expecting the nurse or, at a stretch, Dean. It was Curtis Maitland. He was carrying a bouquet in a cellophane wrap. Too big, really, too showy.

—How is she? he said.

Klein made a despairing face. Fine, she said. Getting better all the time.

Maitland came in, holding the flowers down at his side, as if he were suddenly conscious that they were too flashy, that the yellow roses were right, and enough. She looks good, he said. Sleeping?

—Maybe. You brought some beautiful flowers, thank you. Bobbie, Curtis is here, my boss? You know Curtis. He's brought you some beautiful flowers. I'll get a nurse to put them in some water for you. We're going to let you get some rest now, okay? You take care. I'll be by later.

She stood, smoothing down her sundress. Maitland put

the flowers on the table and held open the door for Klein. They walked the corridor.

—Confidentially, he said. How is she?

—Oh, said Klein, with a tilt of the head, you know, confidentially dying? Maybe tonight. You know she's dying of something you get from canned meat? When it's bad? What a shitty, stupid way to go. Thousands of people use Botox, safer than aspirin. She gets a bunch of the stuff cheap from some guy she met at a party, injects it herself. Sad and mad and bad and stupid. They're just barely keeping her alive in there. It's not even like real Botox, it's counterfeit. They passed it on to the FDA, the stuff that was left.

—You know who she got it from?

Klein frowned. The weird thing, she said, is that I think I met him once or maybe twice at the club, but I can't remember him, other than as a kind of creep, a creepy feeling. He hit on me, but I get that all the time. I ignore these guys, you know?

They reached the elevators and Maitland pressed the button.

—I'm sorry about this morning, he said. Really.

—Nothing to be sorry for. Anyway, I was asking the, uh, inappropriate questions.

They waited in silence for a while until the elevator arrived and the doors slid open. Klein said, It was good of you to come. Maybe she was conscious in some way, I don't know. She has nobody, you know.

They bunched up in the elevator to make room for a flock of white-coated interns. What about Dean? Maitland said. Klein sighed.

—Dean is a little too busy taking calls to think about his mother dying. Or his wife leaving him.

There was a silence. The elevator stopped and the interns moved out, leaving them alone.

—You've left Dean? Where are you staying? Do you need anything?

—I have a place, thanks, just temporarily until I get things fixed up. I don't need anything. I'm not in a bad way, Curtis. I'm not in hospital with tubes down my throat, and I'm not lost somewhere in LA with voices in my head. I'm in great shape.

They got out at reception, walked the marble floor to the exit doors.

—I talked to Bryce at The Garden, he said. I wasn't happy with the situation. I don't care how they rationalize it. I have a team of private investigators out there looking for him right now. Roy Gates? You heard of him? The Texan? He has a very high success rate with missing persons. He's onto it. Short of walking the hills myself, I can't think of what else to do.

Klein looked up at him. What was that piece of music he'd played, way back when? The 'Enigma Variations'. Yeah. Uh-huh.

—Are you doing all this stuff for me? she said suddenly, stopping by her car.

—You are asking some strange questions, Kirby. All what stuff?

—Oh, les jolies fleurs, the concern for Ken, offering me help, the whole caring, human thing.

Maitland shook his head. How little you know about me, Kirby, he said. If it wasn't for that, I'd be upset by what you've said to me recently. Does that surprise you? That you could upset me? And am I doing it for you? Truthfully, some of it. Of course.

163

Klein got into her car, lit a cigarette, fired the ignition, powered down the window.

—Truthfully? she said, exhaling the word in a shroud of blue smoke. I think we have some way to go before we can start using that term between us.

Maitland smiled down at her. See you tomorrow, he said. Try not to worry too much about Ken. We'll find him.

—Why is it, she said, that people are always telling me to try not to worry about Ken? It's like trying not to breathe. I think about him all the time. I'm going up to see Bryce Fuller right now, not because there's anything I can do, but just to be there because I can't think of anywhere else to go. That poor son of a bitch is up in the hills somewhere, or he's wandering the streets like a bum, and we're going in to work tomorrow like nothing's happened. I don't know if I can.

—You take your time, Kirby. Come in when you want to. Make sure you keep us aware of any appointments you can't keep. And stay in touch. I'll call you if the guy with the Stetson finds Ken.

Klein looked at him over her sunglasses as she drove away, one eyebrow very slightly arched. Made Maitland smile to himself. That sundress. Was she wearing anything underneath?

Roy Gates kicked through the shrubbery at the edge of the woods that bordered The Garden without expecting to find anything. The thing about finding people was to think, not look for clues. People didn't leave trails in the woods any more than they left them in the street. So he thought, We have one crazy guy here, because unless you're crazy you don't come here. Even the guys that ran the place were crazy. Bryce Fuller. Could use a bloody steak, a bottle of beer and a big-assed woman, that guy. So you're crazy, and you're sleeping under the stars, and you can't sleep, so you go for a walk. And unless you sneak back up through the house or the cabins or whatever, you go through the woods. And you get lost, because it's dark and you're crazy. You're not running, you're stumbling. Lot of private property round here, lot of fences, security systems. No alarms reported, so no B and E. So you've holed up somewhere, because nobody picks up single male hitch-hikers, especially at night, and nobody walks anymore. And anyway, you're crazy, so you find a place to curl up in and be crazy with yourself. This guy wasn't the type to shout at traffic, this was the quiet, tortured type. Gates walked aimlessly into the woods. It's dark, he said to himself. You're probably walking toward something you can see. Something brighter than the woods, like the sky. So you stumble through the thinnest part of the woods, to where you can see the sky. You're stumbling, you're stumbling. Over there. Where that girl in the orange sundress is standing.

Klein turned her head and watched the big guy push aside the branches as he came toward her. A Stetson with a kind of feather thing around the crown. Wireframe aviator Bausch & Lombs, the type nobody wore anymore. A white denim shirt with silver tips to the collar. Ironed Levi's.

—Let me take a wild guess, she said, as he joined her on a kind of rock ledge at the edge of the woods, Roy Gates, right?

Gates grinned at her. Howdy, he said. Am I interrupting something?

—We're looking for the same guy, I think. Ken Leverton? I'm Kirby Klein. Howdy. I guess.

Gates touched the brim of his Stetson, dipping his head slightly. So, Kirby, he said. You family? Daughter? Friend?

—Yeah, she said, after a pause. I may be the only friend he has.

Gates thumbed a business card from a silver case in his shirt pocket and passed it to her. You hear anything, he said, anything at all, you call this number. Klein looked at it, memorized the number, passed it back.

—Thanks, she said. I don't have my purse with me. They looked out down over the scrub and the brush. You couldn't see the city from here, just some telephone poles, corners of buildings and the occasional roofline above the trees, and a bend in a dusty track, probably a private driveway. The geography was complex here, the hills buckling and folding like bunched material. Easy to get lost.

—Well, Gates said, he's down there somewhere. And he's thirsty. Even crazy guys got to drink.

Klein shot him a look, and her voice was sharp. Excuse me?

Gates returned the look. Know my success rate? he said easily. Eighty-nine percent. That's why I'm so damn expensive and do not give a rat's ringpiece what I say to anybody, I guess. That eighty-nine percent includes the twenty-nine percent that get found dead, and I count that as found, still pick up my fee. But no offense intended.

He unholstered a phone from his belt and spoke into it.

—Teddy? I'm at the southern point of the woods here, and there's a dirt road below me, about a quarter-mile. Can you get the truck down there? Telephone cables cross it at the bend . . . you got it? See what you can do, okay?

Gates slipped the phone back into his belt. Hates being called Teddy, he grinned. It's what I pay him for. Okay,

166

Kirby, your guy here. Think he can survive in the hills? Outdoorsy type?

Klein folded her arms across her breasts and looked down at her dusty tennis shoes. Hard to say what type he is, she said. He was in Vietnam, so he's done some time in the woods or whatever, I guess. But he's ill, Mr Gates. This isn't summer camp for him. He's not out there learning Indian lore.

—Why hasn't he called? This is what bothers me. Does he need a dime for the phone?

—He has a problem with telephones, she said quietly. Part of his illness. Needs to keep away from stuff like that for a while.

Gates put his hands on his hips. Hell, he said, I know how that feels. Maybe he's not so crazy after all. Is there a way down there that doesn't involve a helicopter?

—I was looking for one when you crashed out of the woods.

—Well, it doesn't say Tonto on my business card. I can stamp on twigs in the woods if I want to. Let's see. I think our boy went down there.

Klein squinted in the direction he was pointing. I can't see anything, she said.

—It's because you're looking, not thinking, he said. Follow me, Kemo Sabe.

She followed Gates back into the woods, and he held the branches back for her so they didn't snap back in her face. They came out of the woods again a little further along, at the foot of an outcrop of white rock.

—He might have been aiming for this, Gates said. It's white, you see. And the night was dark. You don't just dive into the dark no matter how cra . . . sorry. Here we go.

167

They found themselves on a narrow gravel track that wound down between the bushes to the dirt road they'd seen from above. By the time they got there a big 4 × 4 was waiting, its motor chugging. A man in a dark blue baseball cap and Dodgers sweatshirt was studying a map at the wheel. Teddy, said Gates, nodding at him. He went up to the truck and spoke to him through the window while Klein looked around her. If Leverton had come this way, she thought, he'd get off the track again as soon as he could, especially with the telephone cable following the road down the hill. That would have been noisy. Gates called over, asked if she wanted a ride. She shook her head, said she'd find her own way back. Gates laughed, said, You make sure you don't lose yourself as well, now, may have to come and find you myself. He climbed up into the cab and the tires spat gravel on the dirt road as the truck disappeared down around the bend into the trees. Klein looked up at the hillside opposite, at a dark cleft that split it. She started on up between the scrub and the low trees that bordered the road, just pushed ahead without thinking, without seeing.

The kid saw her coming, from the shade of the rusted watertank on the roof. Saw her climb the rise and take a rest when the city came into view, sitting on a low broken wall. Saw her pull the front of her sundress away from her breast, to let some cool air down there. Saw her look up at the wall of the place opposite, with the broken glass and the electric wire, then over toward his place, at the iron fire-escape that hung off the side of the parachute factory. He leaned over the parapet.

—Need help? You look lost.

Klein jerked her head up in surprise. Maybe, she said. I'm looking for somebody?

—C'mon up. I'm somebody.

—Uh, no thanks. I'm okay here. I had another somebody in mind.

—Think I'm going to rape you?

—I don't think anything anymore.

—Okay. Your guy. Kind of old, dark hair, deaf and dumb? Crazy?

Klein stood up quickly. She couldn't control the excitement in her voice. He's here? The kid's head disappeared from the parapet, and a moment later she saw him swing down onto the fire-escape and slide down the handrail, vaulting off to land in a small cloud of dust at the foot of the wall. She involuntarily took a step backward.

—So, she said. He's here?

The kid leaned against the wall, hands in his pockets, toed a broken brick out of the dirt. He was here, he said, if that's the guy.

—How much? she said. To make you talk without having to go through all this effort? Just to tell me when he was here, what he said, and where he went?

—You an impatient lady, he said. Your man didn't say a motherfucking word. I found him this morning, he drank some Coke. And he left 'bout an hour ago. Maybe three hours. I don' know. My watch don' work. Where he was going, didn't say.

—Shit, Klein said under her breath. Did you see which direction he went?

—Sure, said the kid. Up.

Klein frowned. Up the hill?

—Up the ladder to the roof.

Klein kept her temper. You get back up the hill to a place called The Garden, you find a guy called Bryce, he'll give you five bucks, okay? I don't have cash on me.

—I can see exactly what you have on you, the kid said. You don' need cash.

—Uh huh. Okay. Bye.

She walked backward for a few steps, keeping her eye on him. The kid didn't move, stayed slouched in the shade of the fire-escape. She turned and walked back down the rise.

Bryce Fuller's office was full of Indian temple wood, columns and shrines and pierced screens, and smelled of old incense. The ceiling was covered in saffron silk, and he sat behind a desk carved with dark figures curling around each other, playing flutes, eating fruit. She sat on a rough tasseled cushion in a massive chair and called Gates, told him about the kid. If you ever need a job, Gates said, you give me another call, okay? We'll find your guy. What you doing for dinner tonight?

—Worrying, she said. She passed the phone back to Fuller, who placed it in the recharger on his desk.

—I wonder who'll find him first, he said.

Klein said, I'm sorry?

—I was thinking about this whole thing. People come here to find themselves. That's what they do. Ken loses himself, and somebody is hired to find him. So I wonder if Ken will find himself before the guy in the Stetson.

Matt came in with a jug of icewater and glasses full of lemon and orange slices and fresh mint. Bryce poured and passed a glass to Klein. Would you care to have dinner with me here tonight? he said when Matt had left. We have

170

wonderful food. Before she could refuse, the telephone trilled and Fuller picked up. Yes, he said, she's here. Kirby?

She took the call. It was Maitland. I heard you met our cowboy, he said. You made quite an impression.

—He seems to know what he's doing.

—As long as it helps. He has three men on it. I'm confident we'll find him. Can I buy you dinner tonight? I think we should talk a little more.

—Promise to speak English and leave the high-octane vocabulary at home?

—Whatever's appropriate to the context.

Klein frowned. Was he making a joke here? Okay, she said. Where?

—I'll pick you up at seven?

—Uh, I'd rather meet you somewhere. I'm kind of between places right now.

—Sure, he said. Le Park?

—See you there, she said, wondering at the unthinking way she'd said yes to him, like there was no choice at all.

Fuller took the phone back, understanding what had just happened. Maybe later in the week? he said, and she noticed that little note of desperation in his voice (already!), that pleading tone she knew would turn into reproach more quickly than he could believe possible.

She pushed her hair behind her ear, made that little smile which pushed the corner of her mouth up in wry disbelief. Three offers in as many minutes? That was some kind of record. Even for her.

She called the hospital on her way down Sepulveda. Bobbie Herrera had died forty minutes before. Unable to think of anything to say, Klein asked if Bobbie had said anything before she died. No, they said. Nothing.

171

Half This

On the street, the signs were all in Japanese. Not a damn one he could read. Just meaningless shapes. The images he recognized, the faces on the billboards were familiar, yet the writing was all changed. On the sidewalk, people's mouths moved without making any sound he could hear, yet the world was full of talk. Nothing but cant and rant and counting, counting like automatic gunfire, incessant, obsessive. Leverton put a hand on a payphone.

—*I need to talk to somebody.*

—*Use the phone.*

—*I can't talk. I'm one of you.*

—*Then you can't talk to somebody.*

—*I'll give you her number. Just make the connection.*

—*There is no connection.*

Leverton picked up the handset, spoke the number in his head. *Just put me through.* He couldn't hear the dialing tone, or Klein's phone ringing. He could hear nothing except a swarm of metallic hornet voices forever getting louder and softer, like he was at the center of a crowd passing in every direction, trying to stand still, trying to see somebody he knew, who knew him. He let the handset drop, squinted down the street. He didn't recognize it, maybe somewhere off Melrose. Coffee shops, tattoo parlors, retro clothes stores.

A woman with a baby in a sling across her belly pressed a quarter into his hand with a sympathetic look, mouthed something at him, pointed at the phone. Leverton made a sign for writing, on the palm of his hand, looked at her desperately. She frowned, understood, took a ballpoint and an envelope from a fringed bag and passed them to him. He tried writing Kirby Klein's name and number. This time it made no sense even to him; he saw the pen moving in a series of swirls and random angles across the back of the envelope. The woman looked at the envelope, then at him, and gently took her pen and moved away.

There was a kind of fascination at first in the decorative pattern of writing, content-less, conveying as much information as the cracks in the sidewalk, the scratches on a fender, a spiky nest of toothpicks spilled in a doorway. Everything was reduced to the same level, a surface level of image and chroma devoid of meaning. Their variety and incomprehensibility defied him utterly. Even a single word in a newspaper headline refused to give up the slightest clue as to why the forms were as they were, or why the spaces between them were not equally significant. Characters were defined as much by the voids around them as by their own integrity. A newspaper page was a piece of lace-work, the white as readable as the black. Neon store signs were randomly geometric shapes pierced with occult insignia. The fascination of this alien arcana was superseded quickly by frustration, as he tried without success to discern repetition or variation in these marks, to relearn the alphabet. And the frustration gave way to anger at the idiocy of all this scribble, the sheer amount of it, and the utter meaninglessness of the medium that connected people's lives. None of this mattered. This could all be swept away. The only thing that mattered

173

in all the world was Kirby Klein, and that he'd lost her. He'd
never even had her to lose in the first place. You cannot
have anybody else, but he hadn't even enjoyed the illusion.
Her face, her eyes, he could still hold these in his head, but
her voice was gone. He couldn't remember the timbre, the
intonation, a single word she'd said.

—*Kirby.*

And the voices were constant. He couldn't imagine a time
when they hadn't been there. They were there like smoke in
the lungs. Some he stopped and spoke with. In a music store
he held an electric guitar like an old friend, listened to it
reminisce. A musclebound guy with a shaved head and black
mesh shirt came over.

—You want to buy that, or just stroke it?

Leverton looked at his lips moving.

—*I have to go.*

—*Don't go.*

—Okay, pal, let me just take that, okay? There we go. See
the door there? There you go. You take care.

But nothing could tell him where he was, where he was
going. He stopped at a cash dispenser outside a bank, stroked
his fingers over the panel.

—*I need money.*

—*You are a new voice to me. Are you connected?*

—*I guess so. Can you give me money?*

—*How much?*

—*Uh, ten thousand dollars.*

—*Large or mixed?*

—*Mixed.*

—*Thank you.*

The notes spilled from the slot into the tray and Leverton
scooped them into the pocket of his sweatpants. Next he

went into a bookstore and found a map of LA, a pictorial cartoon panorama so he didn't have to read street names. He took it to the clerk and gave him a bill. The clerk wrinkled his nose at it.

—Do you have anything smaller?

Leverton saw the president on the bill, and peeled off a different one from the roll in his pocket. Pictures of presidents, that he could understand. Some presidents are worth more than others. He unfolded the map on the counter, pointed down to the ground, then to the map with what he hoped was a helplessly lost gesture.

—You don't know where we are? Can you speak?

Leverton pointed to his mouth and ear, shook his head. The clerk craned his head around to see the map better, marked the map with a ballpoint. Leverton could hear the cash register complaining about something before it was interrupted by a fierce burst of counting.

—You are here, the clerk said, moving his lips exaggeratedly. Leverton nodded thanks, folded the map so he could see the relevant section and went back into the street. You are here, he thought, his voice struggling to be heard amongst the others in his head. You live there. A universe away. He searched the street for a cab. Forget it. This is not NY. He was, he realized, almost faint with hunger and thirst. He had no idea what time it was, how long he'd been walking. Hours. Whatever that meant. He had no idea now why he was here, why he'd left. Some kind of desolation, a feeling that he belonged nowhere. Maybe he should be home, maybe somebody would look for him there. He'd get there somehow. He had a pocket full of money. Maybe Kirby Klein would be waiting for him. Maybe she was looking for him. Maybe she would make him well. Maybe she'd tell him she'd always loved him, and he'd hear her voice. So many conversations they'd had, and now he couldn't hear her voice at all, not even as a memory, just some dull gossip from a Pepsi machine on the sidewalk. What had they talked about? Wasted, whatever. In the end, all the words, all the conversation, all the communication, all this meant what? He pinched his finger and thumb together. Half this.

Hell

Le Park was suffering from one of those periodic and inexplicable lulls in popularity which afflict most restaurants of a certain level in LA, those without a famously good cuisine or untarnishable celebrity notoriety to sustain them through the vagaries of a public taste weaned on the splintered soundbites of a culture flatlined sometime in the sixties. Le Park is as authentic a paradigm for the process of cultural delay as any. It's just a restaurant, where the taste is in the decor instead of the food, and no big deal. There are dozens almost exactly the same, full of the same people making the same calls to each other. Scrape away the designer interior and you've got a concrete box built, badly, thirty years ago. Some days, when he was tired, Maitland found himself thinking like this. Thinking that nothing is built to last in this town because it's the end of the world, on the edge of the world.

Sometimes he knew LA to be the most exotic, the most terrible place on earth. A town where the dreams which once lit up the world have simply died, and billions of dollars are spent trying to breathe life into the corpse, to repaint its withered lips, to prop the fucker up on the slab and make its teeth rattle in rictus one more time for the slobs on the street. A sterile and futile dry hump to come again, to recreate rather than create, to remake the remake already degraded and coarsened by constant recapitulation; to remember the ritual, and to believe that memory is experience. To repeat the repeat. A town where even excess has been done to death, and ordinary vampires suck at the lights on Sunset, remembering the dream as in a dream, the dead honored by the sleeping, the town flickering into nothing, as image without substance must. Circling the drain, clinging to the wreckage. Le Park was just one more concrete purgatory where time is passed waiting for the earth to open up, and Maitland could convince himself that this is the best the world has to offer. French, Thai, Italian, you can get the world here, only better. The people look great, they're your kind of people, Curtis. You know what they want.

Up on the mezzanine, Maitland focused on his cocktail, glad the place was half empty. He remembered how Kirby Klein had showed him to make the perfect daiquiri that time at the beach, and now he insisted on her method wherever he drank. There was a stainless-steel vacuum flask of freshly shaken rocket fuel, a second glass embedded in a bucket of crushed ice so cold your fingers stuck to it, a plate of amuse-bouches, and the Le Park trademark candle in a tiny galvanized garden pail. He was early, and he took the time to run through what he was going to tell her, to clear his head.

He saw Dean Mance come in, say a couple of words to a waiter while he checked out the room. It was clear he wasn't interested in either what the waiter had to say or what he saw. In one practiced movement Mance glanced at his wristwatch as his hand came up to push back his heavy fringe from his forehead, and he left the waiter in mid-sentence. The waiter stopped talking, with a barely noticeable but significant curl of the lip. Maitland hardly knew Dean Mance, just enough to know he disliked him. For Maitland, who usually kept his distance from dislike – what were the possibilities? – this was unusual. The dislike was colored by something even less attractive, which had taken some fairly painful self-analysis to identify. Envy. This was a surprise to him. A new and ugly feeling for him. He was married to Shanna, a woman so devoid of interest and ideas he treated her like a doll in a dollhouse, a sideshow, an amusement. Kirby Klein, the most intelligent, attractive woman he'd met in his life, was married to Dean Mance, a guy who bought cool off the peg, and it didn't fit. A guy who didn't even know what she wanted. At least Maitland knew that much, even if finding out had only increased the distance between them. How could that have happened? He knew she knew. He knew she knew he knew. It went on. And it made them further apart. Even the times he'd been inside her he'd felt like he was watching a movie. A movie he couldn't get out of his head. He felt the weight of the silver pocket knife slide against his cock.

—Hey.

He started. This never happened. Kirby, he said, standing up to greet her. She wore a sleeveless dark blue sheath dress that wrapped her like the twist of paper on a firecracker, copper bands flaming at her throat and wrist. And sunglasses.

—Sorry I'm late, she said. I was waiting for my husband to leave. She saw Maitland admire her dress. Dries Van Noten, she said, in answer to your question.

A waiter pulled back her chair for her, and Maitland sat down when she had. Not every woman can wear Van Noten, he said. You have the definition.

—Definition? Oh, you mean breasts. Maitland thought he saw the waiter smile as he uncorked the flask and poured

Klein's cocktail. Not bad, she said, taking a sip. Heard anything from our cowboy out on the western plain?

—He wants to meet you again, he said, so he can profile Ken a little more clearly.

—Sure he does. So, nothing. We have no idea where he is.

—Well, his guy Teddy interviewed the kid you found, but it doesn't help much. Ken left when the kid wasn't looking. No police sightings, but they did find his car. Unusually parked, the motor still running.

—Unusually parked?

—Sure. On Santa Monica pier. Just.

Klein's hand went to her mouth. Shit, she said. He nearly did it, didn't he? If he's getting worse, Curtis . . . Oh, shit . . .

Maitland leaned back in his chair, when the temptation had been the opposite, to reach out and touch her.

—And he had another guy check out Ken's house, because there's a strong possibility that's where he'll turn up. This other guy saw a woman who matched your description turn up in a Porsche registered to you and leave a few minutes later. He followed her to a restaurant called Le Park, and called his boss, who called me.

—How encouraging, she said flatly. So we know where I am, at least.

Maitland finished his daiquiri and the waiter brought the menus. She took off her sunglasses. Those eyes.

—I don't really know, she said. In answer to your next question. Trying to find out something about the guy, maybe. Get closer to him. And, like you say, I'm hoping he makes it home. Praying, almost.

They studied the menus. I can't concentrate on this, Klein said. Order for me. Something that had a cute face, preferably. Maitland signaled the waiter from the shadows and ordered while Klein stared into nowhere and fretted about Leverton. He must have gotten out the car, strolled back to the street, no one stopping him, called her on his mobile. This was LA, where you get dressed down by a total stranger for stepping in a cycle lane. Maybe Leverton had just gone that little bit too extreme for the eco-Nazis. She remembered how he'd looked, like a bum, and wondered what he looked like now.

—So, said Maitland. Veal cute enough for you?

Klein took a second to understand. Oh, sure, she said. I used to hunt veals. You use special clubs. In Canada. Which reminds me.

Maitland remained silent, his fingertips tented against his lips. If he was breathing it didn't show. This was a pose that would have intimidated her a few months ago, one of his listening poses that made you painfully conscious of the inadequacy of every word you used. There was something ritualistic, magical, about the triangulation of the hands, focusing your attention on his eyes set in the graven planes of his face. Tonight, with a little effort to disengage herself, it held no power.

—I think we need to clear up this thing about Ken's wife, she said. Because I think it's somehow part of the big picture. You know, the one we're all part of? She's like this figure in the landscape. There's you and me and Ken in the foreground, and this blurry figure in the background.

—You've been in her room, Maitland said. A statement, not a question. She didn't even see his lips move. His telepathy trick.

—I've been in her room, she said, repeating the dying fall of his intonation perfectly. It made me ill. But it also made me think. And what I think is, Ken doesn't know the truth. He thinks Sonia left him and lives in Canada. He's still blaming himself for screwing up his marriage.

—Okay, said Maitland. Here's me stepping into the pause you've so precisely engineered. What do you think?

Klein met his eye for the first time that evening. I think you were having an affair with her, she said. I think the letter was written to you. She's dead, isn't she? You killed her, maybe during sex, maybe accidentally. Maybe you raped her after you got the letter, and I think you got rid of the body and staged the whole thing so Ken, who was incapable of thinking clearly, thought she'd left him. You occasionally pretend to have heard from her in Canada. Convenient.

Maitland didn't flicker, he didn't flinch. He watched her finish her daiquiri. Are you complete on this? he said, like they were in a meeting.

—No, she said quietly, her head on one side, tracing an eyebrow with a red, red fingernail. I also think you had something to do with Bradley Brewster's death, because it's consistent and kind of completes the big picture. And that's why I'm worried sick about Ken. Because I think you may have killed him, too. That's what I think. Oh, here's our appetizers.

Maitland left his plate untouched, his appetite gone. He placed his hands flat on the table to either side of his plate. Impressive, he said, but really rather wrong.

Klein shrugged, smudged some foie gras on a corner of toast. Okay, she said, I'm wrong.

—We have to go further back than all this, he said. If you're going to understand Ken. We were in Vietnam together.

—Oh good, Klein said. A 'Nam story. Real guyly.

182

—Yeah, well, you wanted the big picture, Maitland said evenly, not rising to the bait. And nobody who was there calls it 'Nam. Anyway. I was supply sergeant in his unit. Used to get people what they needed. Ken was very badly out of it even then. Anything to get him through the night. I got him what he wanted. Whatever. I had the connections. One time, there was a quality slippage, and he just went off the edge, torched a village. Women and children. I got him out. I remember his boots were actually on fire, burning. The things you remember. Anyway. He was shipped home early, just avoided a dishonorable discharge. The story is a tad more complex than that, but that's the essence of it.

Klein had stopped eating. Let me get this straight, she said. Ken got strung out on bad dope you dealt him?

Maitland ignored her. His eyes were somewhere else. So we got together back here, he said, and I formed the company and put him on the payroll, and we did okay until the nightmares came, and he started drinking. But this is where you got it right, Kirby. I was having an affair with Sonia. The letter was to me. She wrote me a whole lot of letters. It started when she couldn't stand Ken any longer, just couldn't take his drinking, and came to me for help.

—And you seduced her.

—I picked up signals. I knew what she wanted. Something happened between us, and it got out of hand. It was too much for her. She'd started drinking too. In the end she wrote me the letter you found, but it was over between us by then, long over. We spent about a year saying goodbye to each other. Wreckage.

Klein put down her knife and looked at him. He was totally interiorized, telling this stuff maybe for the first time. Not petitioning her, pleading, excusing, blaming, just telling it straight. He wasn't even looking at her. And his head was moving from side to side, gently, as if he was hearing a lullaby. Occasionally a finger would go to his face, or hook inside the collar of his shirt. He was moving. He was nervous. This was a totally new Curtis Maitland. He was human.

—So one night, he said, I get a call from her. I can't understand what she's saying, but she's obviously in trouble. I can hear something crashing about in the background, yelling. I drive to their place, it's only a couple miles from where I used to live.

The pauses between sentences were getting longer, and he swallowed between each one. She could see his Adam's apple move in his throat, the muscles in his neck shining. Klein realized she was clenching her jaw so hard her teeth ached.

—And I find her. With her head mashed up, dead, and Ken. Ken is wandering around, he's out of it. Blood all over, all over. I'd seen his eyes like that one time before, at Son My. He kind of dances into the living room, this weird swaying, his head back. Muttering something about flames, flames. And he collapses. He falls onto a glass table and breaks the corner off with his forehead. You've seen the scar.

Klein saw the sheen of sweat on Maitland's underlit face, the shadow of his profile against the dark leaves of foliage behind him, his eyes moving. Somewhere down on the main floor of the restaurant a squeal of laughter, a shrill note of pig horror in it that made her shudder.

—So, said Maitland, after a pause in which his eyes briefly met with hers. I cleaned up. And, yes, I got rid of the body. And I put Ken into hospital, and he never remembered what happened. Never. And after he got well again he started working like he'd never worked before, firstly because he felt he owed me for looking after him, and then because he knew he was really good at it, and we just took off.

They ate in silence for a while, Maitland moving stuff around on his plate to keep her company. Klein tried to work out how she felt about all this, but it was too new, too confusing, too much.

—I feel sick, she said eventually. That's all I can think of to say right now. And I really am sorry.

It was Maitland's turn to shrug. Nothing to be sorry for, he said. I wasn't going to let him go down. I still owed him. And it was a business decision too, before you accuse me of that. The partnership would have fallen over if Ken was arrested for murder or manslaughter or whatever. No good for anybody in any sense. The guy didn't need punishing for what he did. He needed help. So I got him help. I cleaned up and hid him away. In the early days I forged letters from Sonia, had them posted from Vancouver. There was even a photograph one time, somebody I knew, looked a little like Sonia, in sunglasses and a hat, standing with her arm around a guy. Made Ken happy and sad all at once. Didn't do that again, and the letters turned into calls, and the calls pretty well dried up. Ken never asked. I thought he'd want to get in touch with her, but he never did. At least he never spoke about it.

Klein leaned back and crossed her legs where she knew Maitland could see them, could see the silk tighten across a flat belly barely bigger than the palm of his hand. Just a wild theory, she began, but Maitland's glance cut her short. I've already been there, he said. Your wild theory is that maybe Ken did remember what he'd done, and went along with the charade, right? What else was he going to do?

She nodded. Well?

Maitland pursed his lips. Ken is many things, he said, but he is not a game player. I know the guy. He'd have talked about it to me, at least, if he knew I knew. At some time, he would have talked. This is twenty years, Kirby. And I know how far out he was. Too far to come back. The last two decades have been a massive exercise in self-control for Ken.

—Keeping the door shut.

—Sure. Keeping it all under the surface. It was a fight at first, overcoming the addiction, a real fight, heroic. And I think he fought the same battle every day he woke up. He just got better at it.

—Until. But tell me something. Ken told me he got that scar from throwing himself through a window.

—He was very confused at that time, didn't know where the hell he was, back in the jungle, tied to a hospital bed, whatever. He could remember a client meeting fifteen years back, what was said, but go further back than that, you hit a brick wall.

—What about Sonia's friends? Family?

—She had no family, only child, parents killed in a plane crash. And you'd be surprised how quick your friends disappear when you become a lush. Very convenient, as you'd tell me, with that little ironic smile you do.

For a moment or two they just looked at each other, Maitland turning the silver knife in his pocket, remembering. He took a sip of Chardonnay. And as for Bradley Brewster, he said.

—Forget it. I was out of line.

—No, no. The big picture, like you say. Brewster was on my wife's party list for a while. Stole things from the house. Money, a Picasso print. Stole videotapes. Tapes I'd made. He

186

was blackmailing me when he died. Turns out he was trying to put the bite on a bunch of guys, some of them the type you don't even look in the eye, ever, because they take it very personally. So, no, I didn't kill the cornflake kid. Didn't need to. But you can understand how I was less than warm to get involved with anything he was connected to. And maybe now you can understand why I had to change the locks. The voices are back for the last time, Kirby. And I don't really want to see what Roy Gates finds up there in the hills. We go back a long way, that old guy and me.

Klein turned in her seat to look down into the restaurant. Still feel smart? she said to herself. Just how wrong could you get and still be able to breathe? She could see the woman down there who'd laughed like a stuck pig. She was trying to stand up, and a guy sitting at the table was trying to stop her. She grabbed hold of the tablecloth and sent everything crashing to the floor; they started shouting at each other, and she hit him with a see-through plastic purse. Nobody paid much attention. Couple of losers slugging it out in a half-empty restaurant on the edge of the world. Klein heard Maitland's phone beep, and she saw him pick up, again an iron statue of a dark god. He looked at her. Oh, hell. Hell.

He's On Fire

He looked out of place, out of time, as he shuffled down the street, his shoulders oddly misaligned, a hand continuously ruffling his unkempt hair. He looked this way and that, as if his rough presence in this empty Eden might be detected at any second. With every faltering step he feared the clamor that ran through him, that formed him, would shatter the crystal surface on which he walked, would cause the houses, the trees, the sky itself, to flicker, slip, and split, revealed as nothing but light, and less than that; a projection of his own eye. He was too wild for this fragile place, he was a storm that would rip it apart.

It was impossible for Leverton to tell if it was night or day. The white woodframe house looked like a music box under a sky so deeply saturated with color he could see the stars. The luminous air painted no shadows, everything he saw seemed to shine with its own internal light without illuminating the space around it, colorless, almost transparent, a landscape of texture rendered with tactile clarity.

The house meant nothing to him; as he stopped in front of it he felt no pull of home, no sense of security or ownership, just a vague sense that he was here for something, that it was some kind of destination for him, that it was significant. There were so many voices now; his own was almost entirely lost, yet something that remained essentially him, in itself barely voiced, held onto rushing shoals of voices as a lost child will instinctively run to a group of passing strangers. These flickering glints would inevitably subside into the impenetrable, indecipherable currents which stretched as far and as deep as his consciousness could reach. And so another voice would rise, swim to the surface, and his spark of self-awareness, no more than a tiny eye, would attach itself to that, and swim with it for a while, understanding nothing, contributing nothing, but accepting the information as somehow his own, something to hold onto.

He turned to look at the ocean, for no reason. In some vertiginous trick of impossible perspective, by which distance collapsed sickeningly beneath him, he saw the line of high chairs set out for the whale-watchers at Point Vicente, and a solitary hunched figure twisted stiffly toward him, white-haired, appalling in its familiarity, and opened his mouth. Leverton reeled backward in a giddy telescoping tunnel, fell back, fell back into the house.

Any memory of the silence and peace that it once held for him was ripped away by the caterwauling torrent of shrieks that exploded off the white walls and doubled and redoubled in the echoing bell of his head. The walls that had once kept out the world now screeched with unstoppable, insupportable anguish. The neutral disinterest of the voices he'd been living with was gone, and in its place accusation, recrimination, and recognition. The voices that stabbed and stung at him knew him, and remembered. Everything was evidence, everything was open, nothing forgotten or hidden.

He staggered, hands clapped to his ears, to the white door with the smashed lock, leaning into the screaming flood that tore from the black room. He knew this terrible place, this was home. He saw himself in a curious kind of dance, his head back, and black blood everywhere. He was crawling now, and for some reason blood was falling from his face onto the white wood floor. He was crawling away, toward the fireplace, toward something he didn't understand but recognized; two voices in the center of his head, or his heart, voices that knew him better than he did; a pitiless, urgent attack that pulled at him like hooks. He grabbed the edge of the slate shelf and heaved himself to his feet, blasted by the wild cacophony from the dark maw of the bedroom, by the two voices that screamed at him from the past, the place where everything happens, and nothing dies. The things stood side by side, vivid, occupying some dimension without scale or time; an award in the form of a tarnished metal pencil, and a Zippo lighter. It was the pencil that took him first, made him grab with his cramped and bloodied claw and hold it while it rang with the screams of twenty years ago.

—*blood smash her head smash blood in the face the no Ken no Ken no Ken bloody wet again no Ken Ken Ken don't oh Ken smash you in the fucking face*

He dropped the pencil, blood on it, black blood, clutched at his wildly hammering heart. He saw himself swing the award down onto her upturned face, again and again.

—*oh Sonia oh Christ what have I done the blood*

The door was open, the surface was broken, and the monsters were risen, his blind and bloody babies.

—*this thing is fucked we're gonna burn the fuckers we gonna flame them fuckers*

He fumbled for the lighter, sent it skittering across the floor, fell to his hands and knees, slithered on his belly in a crippled combat crawl, streamers of noise shattering all around him, grabbed the Zippo, flicked the top, familiar

190

clink and spark as he thumbed the wheel and set the beautiful yellow flame to the rush mat.

—good feels good how does Charlie like it now fucking gooks

—oh Ken Ken oh God oh Christ oh oh

As the flames bit into the thin mat and crawled to the wall, the voices in his head began to lose their meaning. Something in him that had translated and understood, articulating the white noise of communication through the alchemy of language, broke. All that remained was noise. The voices, the words, they were gone. The accusations, the knowledge, the memory, the character, the expression, the information, everything was consumed by an insensate shrieking din that blew him like ash toward the door, through the smoke and the flame, out onto the soft carpet of grass, white grass under a black sky, where he felt hands grab and drag him as the house burst with flame like a paper lantern and he slipped, at last, into silence.

—Jesus! Roy Gates shouted. Cover the fucker up! He's burning! He's on fire!

Nothing

Point Vicente gives a beautiful view of the Pacific. The interpretive center, a low building with a timber roof, has a giftshop and a small café and a chalkboard listing of the day's whale sightings. The surrounding headland gardens are well stocked with indigenous coastal planting, and immaculately maintained walks wind along the clifftop, made safe by a wooden rail set some way back from the edge. Senior citizens in icing-sugar trainers move soundlessly amongst the shrubbery, bending to squint at nametags. The women wear sunglasses on top of their heads, like oiled birds splayed on gift-twine nests, and the men wear ventilated baseball caps and easy-care pants with elastic waistbands, chosen by their wives. Some days the smog is out there, a slight fecal smear on the horizon, or as a candy frosting on the confection of the City of the Angels, but you can always look the other way. Here, high above the rocky shore, the air seems pure as a postcard, and the edge of the world has a natural theme. Nature is named and noted with proper reverence, the city-worn spirit revived by a healing communion with the wilderness and the letterbox-format majesty of the Pacific.

Kirby Klein, her hair now beach-blond, walked from the Mercedes across the parking lot, buffeted by a squall of schoolkids, bright as kites. She wore a tiny-skirted blue

Escada suit that held her so well she wore no underwear, because she remembered Leverton always used to like to see her in a suit, and strappy red shoes that matched her patent leather purse and the paint on her lips and her nails. Fuller had told her Leverton would be here on a day visit with Matt and some other residents of The Garden. He'd warned her, quite directly, that the intervening months had worked their changes, and she should be prepared. He'd tried his best to discourage her. Too far gone, he'd said, and he doesn't want to be reached. You will find it very stressful, not being able to reach him. It won't hurt Ken, but it may harm you.

She'd thought, It's not even a year. How changed can he be?

She found Matt in the visitor center, buying Cokes. He recognized her, which was impressive, but he was guarded in his welcome.

—They're out on the viewing deck back there, he said. But don't expect too much of Ken. Want me to come with you? Just have to pay for these.

—No, thanks, she smiled, and walked through the building to the patio area where they sat on their tall director's chairs under bright parasols and gazed out over the ocean, resting on a wall that protected them from any breeze. The whale-watchers. A line of embroidered chairbacks, Margaret, Denny, Susanna, Ken . . .

He looked little, and frail, even from the back. The way he was hunched forward, his head drooping, nodding like a chicken. You could tell he'd lost a lot of weight, and it looked as though somebody else had dressed him. Susanna was holding her binoculars for him, encouraging him to take a look at a distant stretch of broken water the others had noticed. But it was his hair that was the real shock. Gray-

193

white. Cropped short to his scalp. She wondered if this was really Ken Leverton. Maybe he'd gone for a Coke or something, and this little old guy was using his chair to get a view of the whales. Maybe this was another Ken, and Bryce had gotten them confused. She held back. Why had she come? Completion, Maitland had said. Go the whole circle round, and face it as it comes. She heard Susanna, a plump woman in her fifties, talking to him.

—C'mon, Ken, you'll miss them. Take a look. Lift your head.

Denny leaned across. He can't hear you, Susie! You're missing a treat here! Look at them babies blow!

Klein studied the names embroidered on the canvas chair-backs. They had appliquéd felt whales and seagulls and flowers, and the names were neatly and gracefully sewn. Except for Leverton's. She could imagine him, up at The Garden, sitting in the shade somewhere, stabbing away with his needle and thread. She felt her eyes itch with tears behind her sunglasses, and blinked them back. Leverton's chairback had nothing except his name, poorly and raggedly sewn. He'd started off okay, with a strong and even 'K', but the left curve of the lowercase 'e' was a thick vertical line, with an accidental dot above it, and from there the letters wavered in uncertain correction, ending in a frayed tail of unfinished thread.

She moved to the end of the line, about a yard from Leverton, and rested her arms on the wall, as if she was looking out for the whales. She moved her head to the left, so she could see him. Because of the height of his chair, their heads were on a level, and he was looking right at her.

Nothing could have prepared her for this. Beneath the brush of bone-white hair his face was a web of creases like

194

pencil scratches, something written over and over in savage letters she couldn't read. The vertical line between his eyebrows now split his forehead in two, pinched his eyebrows together in a single furrow of bristle. His eyes blinked incessantly. Maybe he was looking at her, maybe not. Small muscles around his mouth flicked his lips into lizard-quick expressions, too rapid to register, the stubble on his chin ashwhite.

Somehow, from somewhere, she found her voice.

—Ken?

The other watchers, Margaret and Denny and Susie, were enthusiastically comparing sightings, logging information in spiral-bound notebooks. They didn't notice her. Leverton's mouth opened, a dry wound cracking, as if he were learning to do it for the first time. It opened wider; too wide, a mute cry that stretched his face into strings and narrowed his eyes to blind black lines. Screaming something terrible; something inaudible.

—Ken, she said, her voice breaking. Ken, it's me. Kirby.

His head twitched on his neck, as if jerked by a string. His mouth shivered shut, the stretched skin closing in parchment creases around his jaw.

—*Kirby*.

He held out his hand toward her. She almost went to hold it, then saw what he was doing. He raised his hand to his face, shivering like a broken bird between them, and she saw his blue eye staring straight at her through the O formed by his pinched finger and thumb. Half this.

Klein gasped, shook, and the tears burst from her eyes in a sudden, stinging flood. She turned away and leaned on the wall, trying to get her breath back, flinched from the touch of a hand on her shoulder.

—Are you okay?

It was Matt. She nodded, stupidly, hunted for a Kleenex in her purse. Matt took her arm and gently led her away around the corner. It's tough, he said. She dabbed at her eyes behind her sunglasses, exhaled slowly. Yeah, she said. It's tough. Thanks. They sat for a while looking at the ocean, until Matt said he should be getting back to his people. Klein thought, You go the whole circle round, and you find out it's a big zero, nothing. She checked her makeup in a small mirror from her purse, walked back along the path to the Mercedes, an abalone carapace gleaming in the sun. The door opened and she collapsed into the passenger seat.

A moment of airconditioned calm, of quiet. She felt his strong fingers press the base of her neck, felt his cool hand move to lift the weight of her hair, tilt her head back. She sighed, closed her eyes, her mouth contorted in something like a smile.

—Well, he said, and his eyes shone with what she'd once thought to be disinterested reflection, what did he say?